PALMARES: Vol. 1

By Gayl Jones

PALMARES: Volume 1: ALMEYDITA

Mexia

Mexia, half black and half Indian, was said to be the concubine of a Franciscan priest, Father Tollinare. It was a rule that Franciscan padres were to take only old black women for their housekeepers, but Father Tollinare had taken a young woman, and not a preto, and so it was said that she was not only his housekeeper but his woman, his mistress. She was beautiful, more beautiful than a caboclo, with dark smooth skin of both the black and the Indian, so that her complexion was like red clay. She was plump but small-waisted, the ideal for a woman then. She wore a black string around her plain muslin dress, to show off her small waist and accentuate her hips. Her hair was shiny like the Indian's, but stood tall and thick on her head like any preto's. Her cheekbones were higher than any I've ever seen, and her large, round eyes were mostly melancholy, but sometimes they'd sparkle. She never spoke to anyone. I had never heard her speak even to the Father. Perhaps if what people said was true, she spoke when they were alone together, at those intimate times, but what if not then? What if she did not speak even at those moments? What of it?

To me she seemed a good woman, and I'm sure she knew the Portuguese as well as anyone in Bahia, better than most. I heard Father Tollinare once call her Silent Spirit.

Father Tollinare lived in rooms attached to the chapel of the casa grande. The walls were thick and white and there was little furniture, only a hard bed, a table, a long rosewood bench, and many chairs. A painting of a long-haired, dark-skinned Christ was on the wall, his eyes large and melancholy as Mexia's. In looking at the painting one is drawn to the eyes first and then outward to the rest of the man. He had long dark lashes, dark curly hair and beard and a high forehead. He could have been a dark mulatto or an Indian. His nose was medium sized and rounded, not sharp and pointy like the European's. When I first saw the painting, I thought the eyes were Mexia's, but then Father Tollinare explained to me that that was the Christ. He didn't explain then that his own Christ was as pale as himself and that the dark one was to better lead us dark ones to Christianity.

I was too young to understand the tale of the priest and his concubine, but no one on the plantation showed any moral outrage toward either Father Tollinare or his woman--it was only outsiders. It is said that once, for instance, two of Father Tollinare's superiors from Rio came to visit and stayed there expecting to be angry and offended, but had ended up developing some attachment to the woman and respected her reserve and dignity. When they left, it is said, they both bowed carefully to the woman and had looked at Father Tollinare with what could only be described as envy. I'd not seen this for myself, but had heard my mother and grandmother and other women who sat about in a hut in the senzala smoking long pipes and talking.

"They looked at her as if she was something sacred," one woman said.

"Yes, and at him with envy."

"It wasn't envy. Priests don't have envy. They don't have emotions."

"Love of God then."

"I'm no Christian. They looked at her as if they wanted to take possession of her their own selves. What're you looking at me for? I'm no Christian."

"What's the matter with her? She never talks."

"But she does no harm to anyone."

"You can see in his eyes how he loves her. Not like a senhor de engenho."

"He couldn't. Priests are only supposed to love God. It's just an evil tale."

"I know a priest who sent his sons to Europe to study."

"Sons did you say?"

"Sim. He can't bear it when she's not there. He has to see her, even if she's silent as a fig."

"I bet she talks to him. I bet she talks to him those times of sim sim sim sim."

"I wonder if she loves him."

"Look at Almeydita, how she's watching with her ojos grandes. Come and sit beside me, menina. What d'you think?"

"I think he loves her."

"She doesn't know what it all means."

"Sim, she does. You know sim sim sim sim. Here's coconut milk and cinnamon."

I was seven and I was a slave. I liked Father Tollinare because he had taught me how to read. He brought black, Indian children, and white ones from the casa grande into his rooms and taught us all together the catechism and how to read from the Bible. Sometimes the woman Mexia would be there, sweeping or making a sweet out of manioc flour. But she never spoke.

Once I entered the room early and alone. Father Tollinare had not come yet. But Mexia was there mixing something with molasses, Brazil nuts, manioc paste, cinnamon, clove and fruit. I stood watching her, and when she finished, she gave me a little bowl of it to eat. She handed it to me with such gentleness, but didn't speak to me.

I learned to read and write between the ages of seven and nine years. I learned some geography and all the Bible stories and lives of the saints. Some places in Bahia not even the children of the brancos are taught anything, so I considered the years with Father Tollinare to be fortunate ones.

Father Tollinare was a tall reinol, born in the Old World, with a high broad forehead and big hands sticking out of the sleeves of his cassock. During the studies, he'd pass one worn Bible around and we'd read the stories, and he'd shake his head when we dropped letters off the ends of words, and he'd say, "In Portugal they say it this way." "But here we say it this way," I protested once. He looked at me sternly. He told me to give the book to Rafael. I did, swinging my legs and string down at the dust on my feet. Rafael read the passage over and put in the missing letters. Father Tollinare smiled and said, "That's the way it should be done." I started to say again "But that's not how I hear them say it in Bahia. The pretos or brancos either." Instead I said nothing. I was afraid that if I spoke a second time, he might scold me and send me out. I was silent because I wanted to know how to read and write the words, even if I continued to pronounce them a different way.

In dreams I would always hear myself challenging him, though.

"If you were in Portugal, how'd you say that?" he'd ask.

"I'm not in Portugal."

"Read that word."

"I don't know it. I've never heard it."

"What's the meaning of it?"

"If I heard it, I'd know."

But mostly it's the woman Mexia who stays in my memory. When I was seven she was the image for me of what it might mean to be a woman in this world.

I remember when I was sitting in the corner eating my bowl of sweet mixture that Mexia had given me, the Father came in and tapped me on the forehead.

"What's good, Almeydita?"

"This is."

"I mean what does it mean to be good? What does it mean to be good in the world."

I looked up at his round gray eyes but said nothing.

"How do you know what is good for life and for the soul?" he persisted.

I admitted I didn't know.

"Do you think you'll find your spiritual place in this world?"

I didn't answer and he tapped my forehead again. Then he went and sat at his long wooden desk and opened his catechism. He had a slender, delicate nose. Mexia left the room and came back bringing him a wash basin and a linen towel. He said nothing to her. He didn't say thanks. He didn't even smile. She handled his big hands in the wash basin, massaged the tips of his fingers and his palms. She looked at him but didn't speak. As I watched her, I could see myself as a tall, silent woman, but I couldn't picture a place for myself. I kept watching Mexia standing over the huge man in the dark cassock. His nose seemed too slender and delicate for his size. I watched them and pictured them in a field of sugarcane. She stood with her back to him. He had his hand flat against her back and was whispering something close to her. At first I couldn't imagine what he was saying, then I heard him say, "Sim. Sim. Sim. Sim."

When Mexia finished washing his big hands, she turned, saw me and looked as if she'd forgotten I was there. I wondered if that was what the

Father meant when he spoke the word "epiphany." She turned her eyes from me and went out.

As soon as the other children came inside and took their seats, Father Tollinare got up from his desk and stood in front of me first with the huge Bible. He said my name several times before I took the Bible and began to read, leaving off the end letters. He shook his head, but this time he didn't scold me. Instead he simply passed the book to a young Indian girl who kept all the letters as she saw them. I felt he must've understood that I could have done the same thing if I'd wanted to. I felt arrogant in my small defiance.

After the schooling, I entered the hut of my mother. The hut was in the senzala some distance from the big house, behind the cinchona trees. My grandmother was sitting in her hammock making a basket. My mother sat in the corner cutting cassava and shelling ground nuts.

I asked my mother, "Do you believe Father Tollinare makes love with the woman Mexia?"

My mother frowned deeply, then she said, "Priests don't make love with women. Priests make love with no one."

My grandmother laughed. "They love the holy virgin," she said. She laughed again. "I haven't known one priest who didn't love the holy virgin."

My mother went on cutting cassava. My grandmother kept laughing.

"Is Mexia a holy virgin?" I asked.

"No," said my mother.

My grandmother laughed again. I looked at her and smiled because people said my grandmother was a crazy woman.

"Hush and come help me shell these nuts," said my mother. "Hasn't the priest been good to you?"

I smiled at my grandmother, then I sat on the ground beside my mother, who pushed the basket of ground nuts toward me.

"Tomorrow we'll go for a walk, Almeydita," said my grandmother, "and I'll tell you all about sim sim sim sim. I'll tell you all about what takes place between a man and woman. I'll take you to the place of the men and women."

My mother gave her a scolding look.

"I'm a crazy woman. I can take her anywhere," my grandmother said.

That night, in my hammock, I dreamed I was Mexia. I washed his hands in the basin but they turned as dark as my own and then he took my little hands in his big ones. His face was still large and red with the delicate nose that quivered and he was wearing strange clothing like the wings of butterflies or some rainbow-colored fish, but his large hands were my color and he kept holding mine in his as he whispered to me.

"Mexia, why don't you ever speak to me?"

I, as Mexia said nothing.

"Why're you such a different woman? Why're you so strange? Why're you so contrary? Why don't you ever talk to me?"

Still I didn't answer.

"You know why you're here, don't you?"

I looked up at his gray eyes.

"Because of all the others I felt that you had a greatness of spirit. But now I'm not sure. Now I'm not too sure. Now I'm not so sure at all. Say something. Eh, you're just a creature like all the others. But I love you. Don't you believe that? I love you so much. Why don't you say something to me, woman."

But I kept standing there, saying nothing. Then his look changed. His nose still quivered, but it was a different sort of quiver. "Well, I'll sell you to Father Cordial. He wanted you. I'll sell you to Father Cordial or Father Conto. I can't abide strangeness."

All that I heard in my dream, although he'd never said a word to her in my presence.

"Talk to me, Mexia," he snorted. Then he said the same thing tenderly.

I remained silent.

"What're you doing here? Don't you know you're a danger? Don't you know you're a danger?"

He put his hand on my shoulder. It was a soft hand, as white as lace.

"Everyday you become more dangerous. But everyday more wary and elusive."

I'd never heard him say a thing to her, nor had I ever heard those words before, yet I heard him say them in my dream, as clear as day.

"Speak to me, Mexia. I know you're an intelligent woman. I know you're not a dumb creature, like the others."

The Place of the Men and the Women

"Tomorrow when you go to visit Pao Joaquim you must say nothing, you must observe silence before him. You must be like a little sphinx, do you hear me? A little sphinx. And he'll give you a blessing."

I said yes that I'd be just like that.

"Today I'll tell you a little tale. Come, help me gather palm leaves for your mother. The priest selected you as one of the bright ones, so you're seeing another little world. You've got nothing to do but smile at strangers and curtsy and let all the women with loose hair lie in your lap while you rub lice from their hair. Isn't that your only little experience in this complex world? Rubbing lice from the heads of white men's daughters?"

I grabbed at the low branches, she at the tall ones. She'd only a string of cloth across her belly. I looked sideways at her hanging breasts and the rippling muscles in her thighs as she reached up on tiptoe.

"And to run with their little chamber pots and to fill the whale oil lantern and polish rosewood. All you'll remember of this age is a big goose-faced man in a cassock and a whale oil lamp."

I jumped when she said "goose-faced" because I'd never thought of Father Tollinare as anything but a big handsome man, except his nose seemed too small for his face, that's all. Well, perhaps he wasn't handsome. Perhaps he was a funny-looking man after all. Then what did Mexia see in him? Did she scratch the lice from his head while he lay in her lap?

"That's all you're remember of this age," she repeated, reaching to a taller branch. "And stories of enchanted Mooresses with charms hidden in their hair."

I grabbed a palm frond and dropped it in my apron.

"Ah, when you grow up, though, you'll wander from place to place, an old storyteller perhaps? But tomorrow, my dear, you must say nothing. Absolutely nothing. You must stare at him with your large soft eyes and say nothing. You must be the truly silent one," she said shaking the palm leaves. She shook one down at me and I stuffed it in my apron. Mine was a tiny apron, almost full now. "He'll give you a blessing." She looked at me closely. "You won't be afraid of him, will you?"

"Afraid?"

"Of Pao Joaquim. You won't be afraid?"

"No."

"Some fear him. They've learned not to fear the old priests, but they're afraid of their own healers."

I looked around in the palm grove. Here as a long bench and a clearing encircled by palm trees. I imagined lovers meeting secretly.

"Is this the place of the men and the women?" I asked, because I'd never been here before and it did seem like a magic place. Now I looked around at it expecting magic. She laughed softly, and sat down on a rock.

"To you," she began, "I seem like an ordinary old woman don't I? But there've been some times in my life when others have seen me with fascination, with enchantment, as if I were invested with some magic, that magic you're seeking now, and I've entered their imaginations."

I looked at her, holding the palm leaves in her own large apron. I didn't know how I saw her. Some said that she was only a crazy woman, but a crazy woman who knew magic, which made some difference. Me, I'd never seen her work any magic.

"Ah, and I've also been a valueless thing. I've had no value for some, while others I've carried through fascination and terror. But listen, menina. The imagination is broad. It ranges. But everything happens in this complex world, and some say it's all right."

Now I felt sure she was playing with me, and I laughed. Because at other times she'd shown me her special craziness in her stories, and I'd laughed. But now she didn't laugh along with me. She looked at me in a hard silence.

"Every woman wants a man who values her," she said and added, "Even in these circumstances. We may be slaves but we don't have to *be* slaves."

I looked at her, my eyes still round with delight, but I felt that in my laughter I'd missed something, that there was something that she'd told me while I was laughing and that this completed it. I wondered why we sat on a mere rock and not on the long bench.

"Listen. I have been everywhere, from Tamararca, to Pernambuco, to Ilheos, to Rio, to Bahia. I'm like cane. I'm everywhere. What you see though is an ordinary woman, a basket maker, but didn't you see me tell Ainda that it was that bone keeping the circulation from her feet? Didn't you see me work on her? Didn't I heal her?"

I nodded because I'd seen Ainda rise and dance the batuque with the others, and in the morning she'd gone to the cane fields with a red rag tied around her head, telling everyone how something had stopped the circulation in her feet for a whole year.

"Didn't I chase the devil away?" she asked.

I nodded.

"And didn't I touch Goncalo's forehead and cure him of his craziness?"

I looked at her. She smiled.

"You want me to cure my own? Ha. Ha. Shall I cure yours?"

I shook my head and smiled and kicked my feet in the grass. I shook the palm leaves in my apron and stared at the distant hills, the dark and green land, one of the ridges jutting out like the head of a green cobra.

"Here we've got the best fruit in the state."

The master and a stranger passed. The master glanced at my grandmother, the stranger at me. I smiled. Or perhaps it was not at us they were looking, but merely in our direction.

"You dry the leaves first, and then you tear them apart, like this," my grandmother said. "And when you're out in the field, you chew on a cane stalk and it'll give you energy...and kill the hunger." The last thing she said softly so the master wouldn't hear.

"Have you found out who's been setting the fires?" asked the stranger.

"Quem e aquele desconhecido?" I whispered.

Grandmother shook her head, but she cocked her ear to listen.

"No, not yet," replied the master, "but mulher or homem…"

He said something so softly that he couldn't be heard.

The two men left the palm groove. I saw the stranger turn to look at me, again. Yes, it was at me he looked.

"I'll show you how to make bowls out of palm nut shells," said my grandmother in an ordinary voice, then she closed her eyes and leaned against a palm tree. "I see a black man sitting on a horse."

"Pretos can't ride horses. It's against the law. I know that."

"Hush. All black men and women will gain liberty here. Between the rocks I see abandoned plantations, but there's a white man lying on a hammock. Oh, there's a white man lying on a hammock, eating a mandacaru."

I knew that only brancos rode horses, but anyone could lie in a hammock and eat a mandacaru but pretos couldn't do it not just anytime they wanted. Abandoned plantations? Freedom? Was that why they called her a crazy woman, to speak always of such things? I stared at the hill that stuck out like the head of a green cobra. A tapir peeked out at me from under a low branch.

"I see people dancing in the streets of Bahia. Pretos and brancos dancing. But there's one old crazy woman going around saying, 'Is it true I'm a free woman? Is it true I'm free?' And an old crazy man comes up to her and says, 'As long as you're with me.' Then they dance the batuque. And there's a white man lying in a hammock eating a mandacaru. There's a white man eating a mandacaru." She sang the lines, then she said, "But me? I'll tell you what I'll remember. A slow whisper without any tenderness and the penitents of St. Sebastian slashing themselves with pieces of broken glass."

"Will you be there on the day of our freedom?"

"We'll all be there," she answered. Then she laughed. "'Is it true I'm a free woman?' Oh, I'll be out in the street with everyone dancing the batuque to the sound of African drums."

I laughed at her. I rubbed the large soft leaves of the palm tree and stared at the hill.

"There're a variety of snakes," she said, as if she'd seen my mind. "I'll show you the magic that can be done with a magical one."

I looked at her and frowned. I looked again at the strange place she'd brought me to, waiting, holding onto the palm leaves in my apron.

"That man behind you," she whispered suddenly, pointing, and learning into my ear. "He's the one I brought you here to tell you about. His name's Rugendas. I wanted to tell you about me and Senhor Rugendas."

I looked behind me, but here was no one standing there. I looked back at her. She was still leaning into my ear and staring back over my shoulder at him. I looked behind me again, but I still saw no one.

"His name's Senhor Rugendas," she said, still looking behind my shoulder, but leaning forward now. "Your mother would remember him. It took me a long time to make any kind of peace with his world or his spirit. But still it's no kind of peace. I did my duties, but I did them without any feeling. You hear me laugh, don't you? But I'm without laughter. I'm an old woman without any laughter. But I have laughed. I have held laughter and fear in the same fist." She picked up one of the palm leaves from her apron and held it in her fist. She shoved her fist out in the direction where Senhor Rugendas was, then drew it back. But still I saw no Senhor Rugendas. "Haven't I, Rugendas?" she asked the man who wasn't there, or whom I didn't see.

She waited though as if he would answer, then she looked back at me. Then she turned her eyes on Senhor Rugendas again. Her eyes threw daggers at him, then she looked back at me.

"Yes, he's seen me hold laughter and terror in the same fist. Rugendas came here feeling that it was a land of promise and wasn't it that for you, mapmaker? But me, I wanted nothing from this place. I'm an old woman without any laughter, but I can still bite blood from an onion, can't I, Rugendas? Yes, he knows I can. See how he loves me and fears me too? He's looking at my breasts now. They're not so high as they one were, Senhor." She moved the upper part of her body; her breasts shook gently. "'You're a strange one,' he told me. 'You're a strange one,' he said. 'No,' I replied. 'I'm like any other woman.' But to him, he couldn't see me as the men in my own country would have. He saw a strange, exotic creature. No, he didn' see me as a full and human woman. 'Pick one and I'll bring her to you. See how quiet she is. She's yours. You hear that? Come to the land of gold and women. They're always open, these women. Do you hear that? Everything comes from God."

She shook the palm leaves again and her breasts gently. The nipples on them jutted out and looked like fruit. "He asked me if I felt like I was a new woman here. A new land, a new woman. No I didn't. Not my land of promise, I told him. I walked with the other women. They let him see me plainly. Didn't you see me plainly, Rugendas? Couldn't you draw a map of me?" She pinched her nipples and they jutted out more. "But it was me you chose. I kept all my feelings away from you. I hid them. A new world for you, Rugendas. A new brave world for you. And this one wants me to tell her about tomorrow. Do you want me to tell her I'm not tomorrow's woman? But I'll be dancing with all the others. I was afraid to be a woman, then, afraid of my breasts and belly. Afraid of the touch inside my hand. I see you laughing. They'd open your mouth so they could look inside. They'd open your mouths and pinch your nipples."

I started to pinch my own nipples, but she struck my hand away. "In those days too I was afraid to look at myself, afraid of my own eyes." She looked at me. I encircled my apron with my hands.

"I'd travel with him. He went around drawing maps and I'd travel with him into the interior of the country. I'd ride behind him on horseback, holding onto his back. Only in the interior of the country. He liked my silence and detachment. I was silent and detached. That was me and he liked that, as he went about his work, his drawings, his calculations. He'd look at me and say all the time, 'The woman isn't talking. Why does the woman not talk.' But he liked it. And me, didn't I stare into the face of the monster. Oh, I don't mean him. By their standards, he's a handsome man. Aren't you, Senhor? I mean the monster of time. Yes, and tomorrow...Rugendas is displeased when I speak of the future. He only wants me to speak of the past. Isn't that so, Senhor?"

She looked at him. I tried to see him but could not. I twisted and turned on the rock, but he was perfectly invisible to me.

"The final act is always an act of mutilation and blood. No? Of recognition and tenderness, he wants me to say. Ha. He knows it's not so. What do I want from you, Senhor? Nothing. What does a woman like me want from a man like you? Nothing, Senhor. I would travel with you, wouldn't I? Lean over your shoulder and study the new maps. You don't want me to leave you? I'm yours anyway, aren't I?"

She leaned over my shoulder as if to listen.

"He says that we're close now, spiritually close. Ha. Do you hear that? That now he acknowledges the spirituality in this creature of God like any other woman. Ha. Hear that? But now he doesn't want me to tell you about the future, and he claims the past too."

She straightened her shoulders and looked at him. Her nipples no longer jutted out. They were rounded. But her breasts were no longer hanging. They were round and firm. Was it magic?

"He doesn't want me to speak of the future and he claims the past too," she repeated. "Do you believe, Rugendas, that a man and woman can be made perfect?" She cupped her hand to her ear and listened. "He wants me to tell him I love him. No, I don't say such things with ease and I won't say them, not to the likes of you, Senhor."

She wrinkled her forehead and stood up. Really, she was not an old woman. She was only thirty years older than me, thirty-seven then, but she called herself an old woman, and my age made me agree with her.

"I've introduced you to Senhor Rugendas," she said, as we left the palm grove and entered the road leading toward the senzala. "Ha. Ha. He feels that we're spiritually close. Spiritually close, did you hear that? Those are his words. He acknowledges my soul. When we entered the palm grove, he said, 'The beautiful woman has come.' Did you hear him? I know charms. I carry charms in my hair. He thinks I'm the same dark stranger I was then. But I'm not the same menina I was when the mapmaker bought me and tried to make me say sim sim sim sim. Did you hear that? Listen. He said he'd be pleased if the old woman would stop talking. That's what he liked in those days, my silence. But I talk now, don't I, Rugendas? Don't I, Senhor? Spiritually close. Ha. Ha. That's for you."

She touched my hair.

"This is my gift to you, Almeydita," she said, as we stood in the road. She touched my hair and my forehead. "And tomorrow Joaquim, Pao Joaquim will give you a blessing." I looked up at her and smiled. "Rugendas. Ha. Ha," she said nodding her head and staring in front of her. We continued walking. "He's displeased when I talk of the future. But I've stood in the face of the monster of time. I've stood in hits face, Rugendas."

I wanted to look back to see if he was following us, to see if I could see him more easily on the road, but I was afraid to. I feared to see him and I feared that again I wouldn't see him.

"Is he a spirit?" I whispered.

"Is *who* a spirit?"

"Rugendas."

"Rugendas a spirit? Ha. He feels we are spiritually close. Ha. Ha. that's what he feels, that's what he says he feels."

I laughed too, stroking the large soft leaves.

"Rugendas a spirit," she kept repeating and laughing. "What maps have you drawn on your new world of the spirit?" she inquired. "Well, perhaps we're closer now in spirit," she added with a chuckle.

Pao Joaquim

In the hut of Pao Joaquim I'm silent. I stare across at him and he stares at me with his strange eyes. I hold my hands in my lap staring at him, then he motions for me to rise and I do. He is wearing a mask. He stares out from it with his strange eyes. As I go out, my grandmother lowers her head and enters. When she returns, she touches my shoulder. "Come and go for a walk with me," she says.

In the road a black man comes riding by on a horse. He sits very tall and straight in the saddle. I've never seen a black man on a horse before, because here it's against the law. So why is he sitting up there? I've never seen a black man sit on a horse before, and I've never seen any man sitting on a horse like he does. He's wearing a white muslin shirt and ordinary cotton pants, cotton they call Sea Island cotton, cotton they call Egyptian cotton. His skin is dark and smooth and he has a beard, a beard like the one on the mask of Pao Joaquim. When he gets to us he stops and holds his hand down. My grandmother takes it and he tries to pull her up on the horse. "No, it's not the time," she whispers.

He sits tall with his shoulders back and says nothing. I think he's looking at me, but can't tell. He jerks the stirrups and rides on. I start to look back at him, but my grandmother holds my head forward and we keep walking. We walk on a flat wide road.

"He always wore a wide hat and he gave me a smaller narrower hat," my grandmother said.

She picked up two small stones from the road to jingle them in her hands as we walked. "I'd hold onto his waist and ride with him that way all the way into the interior. We didn't travel into the city, because then there'd be evil stories, and he thought he could shield me. But no man has such power. In the interior, in the solitude of forest and jungle, that was my place. I was his woman, but I was my own too. He knew I was my own with my own power, different from his compasses and mathematical reckonings."

"Who? That man?" I asked. I wanted to look back, but stared ahead.

"Rugendas I meant."

"And that one?"

She ignored my question. "One day we were riding and I was holding his waist, Rugendas, and the horse was prancing. And we came to this enclosure, like a huge stable, and there was a black man inside sitting on a donkey. He was wearing a vest and no shirt and a wide straw hat and leaning forward with his back hunched. The donkey's ears were pricked up like he was listening for something. Then when the black man saw us--we were well upon him before he saw us--but then when he saw us, he turned his back to us. Rugendas tried to lead the horse into the enclosure. Was it a slave pen? I don't know what it was. A barn or a slave pen out in the middle of the forest. Everytime Rugendas tried to lead the horse in, the horse wouldn't move. Smart horse. He stood with his leg up, with his knee pointed, as if he'd go inside, but didn't. I held Rugendas tighter around the waist. I felt as if there was something inside the enclosure I couldn't see. Something beside the man on the donkey. I couldn't take my eyes off him, the man with his back to us. Now he was sitting straight and tall as an arrow.

"Then the black man began to turn his horse around--yes, in the time we were looking and not seeing, the donkey had turned into a horse. There was a woman with dark eyes sitting in front of the fire looking up at the man on the horse, a white man was lying in a hammock, a black man was leaning against a bale of hay putting the finishing touches on a saddle that he'd made. The white man in the hammock saw us and started rising to greet Rugendas. And the black man turned around slowly, but before he got completely around, Rugendas' horse took fright and galloped away."

We were walking in the wide road between the casa grande and the palm grove, but we didn't enter the place of the palmeira trees where she had taken me before, where there was the man that only she saw. We walked back and forth on the long road, and she didn't speak for a long time, and then as we neared the banana grove where the black men were working, I was sure she was saying things not meant for me. I watched the men bare to the waist and wearing only their cotton trousers. Some worked on the ground while others climbed into the banana trees.

"Then we went everywhere. I could never learn that tongue though. He called me something that meant black girl. Was it the same? Nigger. And it could be said to anyone, not just me in particular, but he came looking for me that time, not just anyone. Mr. Rugendas they called him in his country, not Senhor. Have you seen her?"

"Seen who?" I asked. I imagined myself climbing to the tip top of one of the banana trees.

"I left her with the woman who owns the place. No. I have her papers. What's been done with her? Not just any woman."

She was talking that talk now. I listened, looking from her to the men in the trees, but I could understand nothing. It was all nonsense to me. A peacock strutted near us with its bright feathers.

"No, not just any woman."

"Pavao," I mumbled to the bright bird.

"What place did you bring her from? It doesn't matter. We have a woman here. But Mrs. Dumpling has taken her into town with her. Mrs. Dumpling, the English woman, she told me about all her husbands, all along the way, what this one was like and what that one, but still she was a free woman and always would be, as free as a duckweed. She liked this new country, she said, it was just like her. 'Is that your man, the one that left you with me?' she asked. We saw him, waiting. As we got nearer she kept saying what a free woman she was, rubbing it in you know, because I wasn't. Rub the lice from her hair. Rub rub rub rub. 'Do you want me to buy you from him? I was thinking I'd like to. You're a good companion.'

"But no, he wouldn't sell me because I was the one he was waiting for all that time. And she told him too the country was just like her. And they ate together, while I stood in the kitchen. I watched them from the kitchen. I kept watching them. She was a handsome woman in a green silk dress and wearing a hat with feathers and red shoes. I'd never seen a woman to dress like that, except the whores in Rio, but she wasn't a whore, she was a free woman. She'd look solemn at some moments and burst into laughter at others. She had a space between her teeth, but it didn't distract from her handsomeness, it added to it. Handsome I'll call her, because she was no beauty, not even by their rules. I could tell he found the woman interesting. Oh, yes. And there was wine on the table, which they drank freely. The solemn expression, and then the laughter. She swore something by St. Thomas, but I couldn' hear exactly what it was."

"St. Thomas?"

"Santo Tomas."

"'I ain't always such a reveler,' I heard her say, again solemn. He asked her why'd she come to that country. She was silent, then she talked about all her men, how all of them enchanted her."

"Enchanted Mooress."

"Then Mrs. Dumpling said 'I don't dally, I give myself whole, but not to any every man.' He was silent and she looked solemn for some moments, then she burst out laughing again. She could see me in the doorway, I knew it. 'See how jolly I am,' she said loud where I could hear. 'And I sing like a nightingale.' She sang him a ballad, a *romance,* about the English countrysides and lovers and mystical creatures that appeared and disappeared. When she finished she said she wished God would bless his soul. I thought he'd stay with her."

"Pavao," I said to the bright bird who strutted near my feet. I reached down and touched his feathers.

"I kept thinking when we first rode up to the inn--they had inns in that part of the country--I hadn't liked the eyes of the woman. He was talking to her now and suddenly she just sat staring at him. The innkeeper, watching them too, came up and asked, 'What's wrong with the woman?' Rugendas said he didn't know. But I knew exactly what it was. She just kept staring. 'I don't know,' said Rugendas. 'She just started staring like that.' 'Come and look at the woman,' the innkeeper said. 'She's gone mad.' Someone touched her forehead and the side of her face. Everyone was looking at her, except for Rugendas who was looking at me. A doctor was sent for, but even he couldn't discover what was wrong with the woman. The doctor claimed it was called epilepsy, that she'd had herself quite a fit. Oh, he said a number of strange words for it. But Rugendas just kept looking at me.

"'What weed did you give her?' he asked when we were alone.

"I didn't answer.

"'Is that what you'll do to me?' he asked.

"I was silent. In the morning, she recovered and food was taken to her room, she was quite famished, and Rugendas and I rode into a new territory, where there weren't any inns at all."

"Tomorrow they're going to send me away from here to a negro asylum," my grandmother announced matter-of-factly to my mother and me. She sat in her hammock eating a mandacaru while my mother was spreading manioc paste on banana leaves, and I stood in a corner of the hut slicing bananas. In another corner of the hut were baskets woven from palm fronds.

My mother looked toward her, waiting for her to explain.

"They say I'm the one whose been setting the fires."

My grandmother's own hut had burned down and that's why she had moved in with my mother and me. I couldn't imagine her setting fire to her own hut. One of the fields had burned and they had to put out a small fire at the side of the master's house, the casa grande. One man claimed he saw my grandmother sitting inside the hut while it was burning, and furthermore, he said he saw her light the fire and then go inside and sit. They might have believed the first part of his story, if it had not been for the second. He was sold with some slaves on their way to North America, for the crime of telling lies and my grandmother was brought to the hut of my mother. Then a canefield burned and next one side the master's house.

The next day they put my grandmother into a wagon. I ran up to her.

"When I first came here, I was a crazy woman," she explained. "They said when I first came to this land I was crazy. Ha Ha Ha Ha. They wanted to put me into a negro asylum then. Now look at me. You have to be crazy in this land."

She kissed my forehead and jaw. My mother came up behind me and held my shoulders and kept me from plunging forward, into the wagon too.

A Disillusioned and Sadistic Man

When I saw them together, it was as if the dream had stepped out of itself and plunged into the world. They stood with their backs to me, and so instead of coming out into the clearing I squatted in the bushes. She seemed taller than him, her back broader and darker than it had seemed whenever I'd see her inside the chapel. He held his hand, as I remember, fist against her back.

"I beg you to understand," he was saying. "I'm not a sadistic man, I'm a disillusioned man. I beg you to understand me."

She did not answer, nor did she turn around. Was it really her, I wondered then, or was it some other woman? No, the muslin, the small waist.

"I don't know what kind of woman you are," he said with anger, his hand still on her back. "You've become a symbol of something to me. You're like a religion."

She said nothing.

"Why do you make me say absurdities? I enjoy no favors, none, except what the eyes see."

He put his hand against her small waist. The other hand disappeared in front of her.

"What will you fix for me tonight, Mexia?" he asked. He looked like a man in fever, but it was a fever that he relished. "Something with a fine flavor, something made with almonds and lots of sugar and lots of cinnamon…" He sniffed at her hair as if it were that sweet thing. "I'm not a sadistic man," he repeated softly, whispering against her back. "You won't make any sound, will you? Nothing. Something smooth and mouth-watering and full of flavors and yams and meat. I know it's you who's been setting the fires. Some delicacy to preserve a man's spirit. Something wholesome and delicious. I'm disillusioned. Rolls with jelly mango, coconut. I know it's you who's been setting the fires. I know it's you....I wanted you to come out and enjoy the air with me, but always you're silent, and you begin to disappear. I can't bear to have you away. You're like some rare, nocturnal bird. Why do you lead me to say such things? You're a woman of nobility and dignity and energy. Mexia, ah Mexia, Paixao. These are the rules of the game? But there's an exception to every rule. Estas são as regras do jogo? Não há regra sem exceção. Ah, Mexia, no harm done, is there? I'm not a sadistic man, I'm disillusioned. I know it's been you setting those fires."

As she was about to turn, that was when I fell flat on the ground. When I raised myself up again, they were gone. After that, she seemed even more mysterious too, and there was a mingling of fear mixed with affection for her. For him, I felt suspicion and pity. But I told no one it was her setting those fires.

And still sometimes at night as I lay on my hammock, I'd make up my own conversations and actions for them, but always they'd have their backs to me.

"Am I more understandable now?" he'd ask.

Silence.

"I'm not a sadistic man, I'm a reminiscent man."

Both words I'd heard, but I didnt' know their meanings.

Silence. He touched her small waist.

"You're so callipygous."

I'd seen the word once in a romanceiro. Father Tollinare took the book from me and handed me a catechism.

"I like the way you're constructed. I like a woman built just so."

Silence.

"I tell you you're not a wench, you're a lady. Your Negro and Indian ancestry is not imaginary, but that's got nothing to do with worth. It's insignificant. You belong to the better class of mulheres."

Silence.

"I like the aroma of your hair, like cinnamon."

Silence.

"Will you fix me coconuts and oranges, mangoes and cacao, yams and cinnamon, and coconuts, coconuts, coconuts, coconuts. Mexia, you're a sacred being. I don't have the same feelings about color as the other senhores. To me you're a sacred being. Perhaps it's my theologic upbringing and my...the fact that I'm from the Old World. Please forgive me. I'm a disillusioned man. Why do you keep so quiet? Why are you such a danger?"

At this point in the dream or daydream, whenever she'd turn I'd wake up. But somehow whenever I saw the woman, I'd stand in affectionate awe of her, and yet feel at the same time that she was dangerous, "spiritually dangerous," a phrase I heard Father Tollinare say often. How all those words entered my dream I don't know.

"I know you've been setting those fires," he'd whisper against her hair.

The Book Room

There was a room in the back of the one we learned to read in. I used to imagine that it was the room where Mexia and Father Tollinare spent time alone together and where she talked. Once I dreamed that I opened the door of the room and instead of finding Father Tollinare and the lovely Mexia there, I discovered the ugly sea monster hipupiara with his sharp teeth and pointed ears and claws. I stood still, almost as if I was in a trance, unable to speak or scream, staring at the water devil, who had large, almost human eyes but a horrid pointed animal's face, breasts like a woman, but the rest of him a hairy fish. And then Mexia placed her hand gently on my shoulder and pulled me away and shut the door. I knew it was Mexia even though I did not turn to see her. The animal brayed behind the closed door.

"Come away," said Mexia. "You're not the captain's son, you're his slave. Do you think you're Baltesar?"

Baltesar Ferreira, the son of the Captain of São Vicente, had killed such a monster over a hundred years ago. My grandmother had told me the story of the water devil who ate the secret parts of children. Of everyone, but especially he liked the secret parts of children, she said. "They killed one in 1564, but do you think that was the only one? Do you think in the big, mysterious sea there was only one hipupiara?"

I found a sword in my hand and shook Mexia aloose. "I may not be the captain's son, but I'm as brave as he!" I declared and opened the door, but the monster was gone.

But on waking from my dream I was not so brave, and the dream kept me for a long time from discovering what was behind the door, until one day when I was there early, and both Mexia and Father Tollinare had left the room. So I dared to open the door. But there was no monster, only walls and walls of books, more books than I'd ever seen or imagined in the world. Then it seemed so to me.

I walked down the two wooden steps, entered the room and turned in circles. Shelves and tables of books. I lifted one and then another. Among the titles were: Robert Boyle's *The Skeptical Chymist*, Rene Descartes' *Discourse on Method*, Galileo's *Letters on the Solar Spots*, Moliere's *Le Misanthrope*, Milton's *Paradise Lost*, John Bunyan's *The Pilgrim's Progress,* Gine Perez de hita's *The Civil Wars of Granada*, Miguel de Cervantes' *Don Quijote*, Soror Maria Agreda's *Mystical City of God,* Pero de Magalhaes' *The Histories of Brazil*. There were so many books I can't name them here, but there were hundreds of volumes, not only in Portuguese, but in French, Italian, Latin, Greek, and English. I opened the book by Magalhaes to see what he said of our country, but on the very first page I read the following:

"I have read the present work of Pero de Magalhaes, at the order of the gentlemen of the Council General of the Inquisition, and it does not contain anything contrary to our Holy Catholic Faith, nor to good morals; on the contrary, many things well worth reading. Today, the 10th of November, 1575.

Francisco de Gouvea"

And beneath that was written:

"In accordance with the above certificate, the book may be printed and the original shall be returned with one of the printed copies to this council, and this decision shall be printed at the beginning of the book together with the above certificate. At Evora the 10th of November. By order of Manuel Antunez, Secretary of the Council General of the Holy Office of the Inquisition in the year 1575.

I stared at the approbation almost as long as I'd stared at the monster. Then as I began to read the verses and the prologue to the reader, I felt a hand on my shoulder. I turned to look up at Mexia whose look was solemn, worried, afraid. She took the book from my hand and put it down on the table, then she drew me out of the room and closed the door.

"Those aren't for you," she said softly, the first line of words she'd ever said to me. "If Father Tollinare had found you, it'd have been your time of troubles like it was mine."

"Did Father Tollinare find you in there?"

"Yes." She looked down at her fingers.

She sat down on a bench and I sat down beside her.

"What did he do to you?"

She wouldn't answer, but continued to stare at her hands. Her fingers were very long and delicate, but the fingernails were short and ragged.

"I want to read more than the lives of saints," I said.

"So did I," she said gently.

"Do you suppose if I asked him kindly, he'd allow me to read some of them."

"You wouldn't understand most of them," she said.

"Well, I'll learn to understand them," I protested.

"Not so loud," she whispered. "If he ever knows you were there, there'll be trouble."

I pouted. She stroked my head.

"Even he thinks the books are dangerous."

"Like you."

"Like me? What like me?" she asked.

"Dangerous," I said.

She clucked her teeth. "Some of them belong to him, but others belong to his uncle, Father Froger."

"Then I'll ask Father Froger."

"He was burned over fifty years ago in France, for witchcraft."

She was looking at me oddly now, but when I caught her at it, she looked away.

'What did he do for witchcraft? How can a holy father be a witch?"

She looked as if she wanted to laugh.

"I don't know the whole story," she said. "Perhaps he was angry only because when I was in there I discovered the wrong book. There are right books and wrong books. The one I found was an unpublished book by his uncle. He talks about witches, but claims that there are no such things, that witches, or rather the things that witches declare they do and see are merely the hallucinations of melancholy women. That's why they burned him, as a witch and a friend of witches. That's why Father Tollinare..."

I waited, but she wouldn't continue.

"Do you think his uncle was a witch?" I asked.

"He was a strange and different man, that was his only crime," said Father Tollinare entering the room and spying us. But he didn't look at me, he looked at Mexia with hard eyes. "One can believe anything, no matter how impossible."

He kept staring at Mexia as if he were trying to discover something hidden at some depth. With a look of fright, as if it were he the sea monster hipupiara, she got up, holding her skirts and ran. She wore a full dress, like the brancas. Father Tollinare looked at me fiercely, then threw the book he was carrying down on the bench beside me. It was the life of Saint Mary Magdalene, the beautiful woman who washed the feet of Jesus. I'd already read the book many times. It was illustrated, but the Christ inside of it was a white man with blue eyes and blond hair, not like the man on Father Tollinare's wall. But my grandmother had already explained to me by then that the Christ on the Father's wall was to attract the Indians and Negroes to Christianity. "Either that," she declared with a laugh, "or the white one in the book is to attract the Englishmen and Frenchmen and Dutch and Finns to it."

I stared at the long-haired penitent kneeling at the feet of Christ. Did I hear him whisper, "Why are you crying? Don't you think God knows who to bring together? Don't you think he knows what to arrange?"

I sat there in silence, for it was then that I discovered places that Father Tollinare would not allow me to go in my learning, and I wondered what my real education would have been if he'd allowed me to be alone in that room of books.

The next time I tried to get into the room, the door was locked.

"Almeydita, you sly one, read from the life of Saint Mary."

I began, "To know what great love is...."

Lorraine Alsace

"Do they burn witches here?" I asked my mother.

"What do you mean burn witches?"

"Mexia just told me that Father Tollinare is the nephew of a priest they burned for witchcraft."

My mother gave a short hum. Sitting in the corner of the hut, she wove a large hammock with cotton threads. I had taken over the task of weaving the baskets from palm and banana leaves, and sat on the floor with one between my knees. I wondered whether my grandmother was weaving baskets at the negro asylum. I'd asked my mother about the place but she'd refused to divulge any information. I knew that there were many negro asylums scattered about Brazil because slaves were always going "off" in one way or another. Slaves who weren't crazy, but simply intractable were sometimes shipped off to a negro asylum. Sometimes, I learned later, women slaves who were "unapproachable" were sometimes sent there.

"Mexia talked?" my mother asked.

"Yes. But I think she got herself into trouble. I never saw Father Tollinare look so angry."

"Priests get angry. But the son of a priest burned for witchcraft."

"Nephew."

"I bet he's the son," she mumbled.

Then she gave a short hum.

"In England they hang them," she said.

"What do they do here?"

"The Portuguese, eh the Portuguese, they don't do anything, here or in Portugal. They're like the Spanish. They're too busy hunting Jews and Moors. In Spain, a witch wears a Jew's hat."

"Are we Moors?"

"We've got a touch of Moorish blood. We're Sudanese with a touch of Moorish blood."

My mother gave another short hum.

"Is grandmother a witch?" I asked, for that hum sounded exactly like hers.

"A witch?" she repeated.

It was then that grandmother peeked her head in the door. I'll swear it's so, but mother says I was merely daydreaming.

"A witch? I wouldn't be a witch," she said. "A sorceress is the thing to be. A witch is nothing."

"Mother, don't talk so," my mother said, but she swears it's not so, that I was merely daydreaming.

But I remember it exactly like that. I kept looking at my grandmother. She winked at me. She said, "But a curer of those who have been bewitched is the best to be."

"Belief in witches is unchristian," said my mother.

"Well, I'm no Christian," said my grandmother. "Old or new." Then grandmother laughed and hummed. "Witches is how Christians settle unsettled times."

I asked her what she meant.

"May I tell her about Lorraine Alsace?"

"I don't believe there was such a woman." She looked at her mother, frowning then went back to twisting the cotton threads, her fingers quick and agile.

Why does she insist it's not so?

"The hallucinations of a melancholy woman," my grandmother explained and winked at me. How could she have known?

"Your mother doesn't believe anything," she said to me. "Doesn't she know there are things in this world which she hasn't seen and doesn't have any knowledge of. Doesn't she know there are wonders in the world, strange and frightful wonders."

"I know the difference between possible and impossible things," said Mother.

"Would you say it was impossible that the horse trader could have found you again, without my magic?"

My mother bit her lip in silence. I looked from one to the other. Was that why she insists it's not so, because Grandmother mentioned the horse trader? She lifted up the hammock she was making. She pulled on it to test how strong the threads were.

"Alsace," I said to remind my grandmother of the tale she promised.

"Alsace was a Moorish woman who turned up in Bahia de Todos os Santos many years ago, a traveling woman, an itinerant singer and very beautiful. I was a young woman myself then. As soon's she showed up many strange things began to happen. But only natural things, heavy rains, storms, fishing troubles. But because the woman was there and from one of the dark corners of the world, they blamed the occurrences on her. Then one night someone claimed they saw her rubbing devil's grease on her hair and body, and they captured her and imprisoned her. When she was in prison, a guard swore that he saw a big, black bearded man in the cell with her, kissing her on the lips. When she was confronted by the fact that the devil was in there, she told them, 'Indeed, there was no man there, but if one was, wouldn't it've been natural for him to've been a black man with a beard?' They took that to mean a confession that the devil had indeed been with her. I myself was standing on the street when they were taking her to be executed. I myself. She saw me and touched my hand. I was standing on the street, because I'd been sent by my master with some ambergris for…"

"I don't believe the woman passed on any powers to you, Mother. Don't tell the 'nina that."

"The horse trader's here, isn't he? Didn't he know the exact place and time?"

My mother was silent.

"How was unsettled times settled?" I asked.

I'd stopped weaving the basket to listen. Now I sat up in my hammock that had become too small for me.

"Ah, after her execution, there were more heavy rains and storms and fishing problems, but there was no Moorish woman to blame for it, so they blamed it on the laws of nature."

"But your grandmother claims that she caused things this second time, with powers that Alsace had passed to her."

"She was only the medium of the gift, not the source of it."

Mother hummed then she said, "I don't believe she was here. I don't believe in Alsace, because they don't let Moors in the country."

"Don't you think she'd have her ways."

"Did the black bearded man come to you?" I asked. "Is that the one we saw?"

"What black man?" My mother looked at her. My grandmother jumped in the air with excitement.

"Your mother doesn't believe in the invisible world," she explained, "or the powers of anyone except the Portuguese and the Dutchmen. Maybe an Englishman or two." She twisted her hands in her hair and went out.

I swear it's so, but Mother swears it's not. She does say I asked her about the witch and the black man.

"We saw a black man riding on a horse," I told her. "Who is he?"

"It's not for you to know," she scolded. "Some way she's gotten you to share her visions."

"Then she *is* a witch!" I exclaimed, clapping my hands.

"Hush. Come here and hold this."

I went and held the new hammock while she twisted the cotton threads.

The Gathering of Turtle Eggs

But the girl with the turtle eggs, she said was real. It was before my grandmother had been sent off to the nego asylum. We found this young girl. Years later, when I saw my grandmother again, she told me that the young girl was Alsace, come round again, but then I only knew that she was brought to my mother's and grandmother's hut. She was found wandering alone on a beach and she was very sick. She was very thin with dark skin and glossy hair and huge black eyes, and indeed did look like the enchanted Mooresses in the storybooks. My grandmother--did she recognize her then?--placed her in her hammock, but with all her magic she couldn't determine what was wrong with the girl--or refused to tell us. Anyway, my mother went to the man who'd found her and asked him where she was and what was around her when she was found. He said, "On the beach, just the beach. Piles of sand and bits of rock and little dead fish and a basket of broken turtle eggs."

Grandmother came back and said that maybe the girl had been with a crew who'd been gathering turtle eggs.

"To eat?" I wrinkled my nose up. I liked nothing with turtle, not even turtle soup with garlic.

"No," she said. "They make oil out of it. Turtle butter. Very expensive and very good. She must've been traveling with them, the poor dear, and got sick and they left her behind."

She treated the girl not like some stranger, but someone she knew. I didn't know the tale of Alsace at the time though and Father Tollinare didn't believe in reincarnation, claiming it to be a devil's trick. Anyway, the girl stayed with us till she got well. My grandmother never discovered what it was she had, or never told us. She just gave her soups, even turtle soup, and herbs till she got better. But the girl never spoke and she'd back away whenever anyone but grandmother came near her. Even when my grandmother would hand her a plate of rice and bacon she would go into the corner and away from everyone and eat it. Her eyes were as shiny as pearls. I saw her touching my grandmother's hand, but I didn't give it any significance then. I thought it was merely to thank her for the help she'd given. Did my grandmother need more powers? New ones? Was that why Alsace had come again?

Master Entralgo--some people swore behind his back that he was not a branco but only considered himself to be one--sent someone to inquire of the health of the girl. When she was well, he said, I was to bring her to the master. And so when she was well, she walked with me in silence, and kept her arms folded.

"What's your name?" Entralgo asked.

When she didn't answer, I spoke up for her. "I don't know her name, Sir," I said. "She's spoken to no one."

"I'm asking *her* what's her name."

She refused to answer.

"And how'm I going to tell if you're dangerous or not?" he said with a snorting chuckle, "if you don't speak."

The girl still refused to answer, her hands hugging her arms.

"Whose slave're you then?"

No answer.

He watched her with annoyance. I thought he would swoop down and strike her. "Well, if you belong to no one else I'll take you."

"I belong to *me*," she said in a little voice.

He laughed. I waited for him to swoop down on her.

"And did you belong to *you* before *we* found you?"

The girl wasn't much older than I myself, perhaps ten. But I liked her. No one had ever spoken to Engralgo like that. Not anyone I knew.

"Where're your free papers, wench?"

She said nothing. Wasn't she too young to be a wench?

Still she didn't answer, and still I expected him to swoop down on her with his anger, but he merely laughed. Why? What power did she have? I had no idea that this was Alsace.

"You're an uppity little wench," he said.

"I'm not from the same world as you," she said.

"And what world do you come from, wench?"

I kept staring at the girl, who was looking at him directly, not out of the corner of her eyes, as I only looked at brancos.

"If it's the devil, then he owns you," said the man.

"No, I'm from a place there." The girl pointed eastward.

Entralgo said, "Take her back to your grandmother till I decide what's to be done with her. A negro asylum for this one, I'll guess."

The girl turned a moment before I did. I'd been expecting him to swoop down on her, but he hadn't. Whatever he planned to do to her, I wasn't sure, but I knew he planned something. The girl and I walked back. I wanted to ask her why she behaved in such a manner, but I didn't dare. When we got back to the senzala to our hut I told my mother what had taken place. She shook her head and clucked at the girl, saying that it was a wonder Entralgo hadn't stripped her bare and beat her there and then. When I told my grandmother what had happened, she merely looked at the girl and smiled.

Now I was sure that since she'd spoken, she'd continue to speak to us, but she didn't. She seemed more withdrawn than before, taking her food into a corner away from us. She spent whole days alone and in silence. I kept waiting for Entralgo to decide what to do with her. When he did not my mother began to give her bits of laundry to take down to the stream and wash, which she did expressionless.

And when I took her to school with me, Father Tollinare had started to pass her the catechism, then realizing that she was not a regular student, was about to take the book from her, when she took the book and began to read, quickly and intelligently, as if she'd been born to it. She read in a manner that Father Tollinare much regarded, leaving all the endings on all her words.

"Where'd you learn to read like that?" asked Father Tollinare, in amazement.

The girl hunched her shoulders but didn't answer. Mexia, who'd been in the room, had stopped and looked at the child.

"That was wonderful," said Father Tollinare. I'd never heard him make over anyone so, not even the brancos.

Although I was said to be a quick and agile reader, still Father Tollinare complained that I exaggerated some of my words while leaving whole syllables off of others.

"That is perfect, child," he said. "What's your name?"

"She doesn't have a name," I answer quickly. I don't know why I said it. It just popped out, as if someone had impelled me to.

Father Tollinare looked at me with impatience, then back at the child.

"I am called Selvagem," said the girl.

"Savage! Who'd call you that? You're very intelligent."

"She's from Sudan," I said quickly, before she could say anything. "From East Africa."

Father Tollinare looked at me. You could say that I was looking at myself too, for in truth I didn't know a thing about her.

"I want you to come here again and again," he said to the child. "Do you write?" he asked eagerly. "Do you know how to copy the scriptures?"

The girl nodded. Father Tollinare clapped his hands. "But come tomorrow and show me what you can do. I can see you're a very intelligent little girl."

She came the next day and copied the scriptures, but Father Tollinare scolded her for putting things in there that weren't there. She kept putting things in there that were...well, forbidden. He couldn't understand why she didn't copy what she saw. What it was she put into the scriptures, he wouldn't tell us, but he began to look frightened by it, and quickly took the writing papers away from her and tore the papers up.

"I can see you're very intelligent," he proclaimed. "But such things are forbidden. Such things are dangerous."

"That part and that part are my own creation," she said.

He extolled her intelligence, but he said again that such things were forbidden, were dangerous, and were unholy. He told her what was in the scriptures, and if she saw anything else there, why she imagined it, or it was the work of the devil. The girl replied nothing, but she didn't return the next day nor the next; she refused to speak to anyone and drew further into herself.

Once I asked her what turtle oil was used for and she said for light. I asked her if the ship she'd sailed on was a pirate ship. I'd heard tales of pirates.

"Your master was he a pirate?" I asked.

She'd come with me to the palm grove where we gathered palm leaves. She didn't answer, but looked at me as if I were a fool to ask such a question. But I liked her anyway.

And grandmother treated her with a special kind of tenderness. Once she commented that if the girl were from anywhere it was from her own country because there it was considered a virtue for a woman to be quiet, but she admitted that now in this New World she didn't consider silence very virtuous among women. "Ah, but then wasn't I the truly silent woman?" she said. Was it Rugendas she spoke to?

The girl's eyes seemed to get larger whenever my grandmother spoke to her. I knew now it was because grandmother shared the secret of her identity. That is, if she'd to be believed. I know my grandmother would stare at her often. "What should we do?" she'd ask. I thought then that she was asking what we should do with the girl, because she couldn't be fathomed. But now I suspect that she was addressing the girl. Once when she asked that, the girl came and kissed my grandmother as if she recognized her suddenly, then she went out into the yard.

When the girl didn't return for a time, my mother went out to find her. She found her, she said, but she didn't bring her back; she took her instead to Father Tollinare. My grandmother said that she'd committed suicide, that she'd eaten earth, so much of it, and in that way had committed suicide. Some others believe that it was Entralgo that stuffed her with earth and killed her.

"But why?" my mother asked, believing I suppose the first thing.

But my grandmother was again the truly silent one. She refused to explain, nor did she tell us who the girl really was, but when we were alone she told me that that was the way that lessons were learned in the world. I had no idea what she meant.

Antonia Artiga

I suppose the first thing was true, because when Master Entralgo discovered he couldn't have his way with the girl, he took things out on Antonia Artiga. Everyone said she was a drunkard and a thief, although what she stole or continued to steal I don't know. My grandmother swore that it was one thing she stole and only one thing, but that Entralgo (she never called him "Master" not even when speaking face to face with him), but as soon as he learned about the girl, Entralgo beat this Antonia Artiga. It wasn't as if he hadn't beat her before. He'd always beat her for this one thing she'd stolen as if she'd stolen it again and again. And if anything else drove him to annoyance, he'd beat her for that too.

We were sitting in the palm grove where Grandmother had first spoken to the invisible Rugendas. This time, however, she spoke to no one. We sat in silence until we could hear the woman scream. It was loud and long. That's the way she'd do it. One loud long scream and then she'd be silent for the rest of the time. He'd beat her publically, once a week, and like I said, any other time that he was irked. The rest of the time she'd go about her work in the cane field, like any other woman. In the evening she'd sit in front of her hut, sitting very straight and proud, chewing on a canestalk and drinking rum she'd made herself. Then she'd commit some crime again or someone else would do a thing that riled him and he'd go and grab Antonia.

After her beating, my grandmother would visit her or some other woman who knew about medicine and rub salve on her wounds, then the next day, early in the morning, she'd be out in the fields cutting cane with the other women, as if she'd never been beaten.

"What did she steal? What does she keep stealing?" I asked.

"She doesn't keep stealing. What she stole she only stole one time. Such a woman only needs to commit one crime. He goes on beating her for the same one. But that's not why he's beating her now. A man like that can take one reason or another."

I looked at her, but she wouldn't explain in words that I could understand. After a moment, she got up and began picking certain leaves, and then I followed her out of the palm grove and among the cinchona trees. She scratched off some of its bark and drew sap from it.

"Come on," she said. "I'll go see about her. She's more stubborn than a goat, but a man like that can take one reason or another."

I walked beside her up the road. We stood in the senzala watching while they untied the woman from a post. My grandmother left me standing there and walked with the woman into her hut. I went into my mother's hut.

"Why does he beat her in public?" I asked.

I knew he beat other women, but none of them in public. Besides Antonia, only the men were beaten in public. When my mother didn't explain, I climbed into my hammock.

After a long moment, she said, "It's considered indecent to beat a woman out of doors."

I waited for her to explain further, but she wouldn't, as if she wanted me to make the connections she refused to make. "Make the understanding for yourself," was a phrase I often heard my grandmother say. But I sat there with my mouth open waiting for her to make the understanding for me.

Grandmother came in smelling like cinchona salve and told me to shut my mouth before I swallowed a goat.

Entralgo Comes to the Medicine Woman

"He keeps promising her he'll ship her to Corricao's," said Grandmother as she climbed into her hammock and took up a basket to weave.

I shuttered, because I knew that Corricao's was the place where they breed slaves. A few of the slaves on our plantation had been born at Corricao's and disgusting things were whispered, even into the ears of children. I started to ask Grandmother why some slaves had to work harder than others, and why some were even forced to do disgusting things. Perhaps Corricao wouldn't buy Antonia, I was thinking. Perhaps he wouldn't buy a drunkard and a thief, as she was called.

As I was about to speak, a tall house servant loomed in the doorway. I eyed him because they had just started talking to me about going to Pao Joaquim and I knew that Pao Joaquim could be any of the men, behind his mask. But this tall house servant didn't look fierce at all. Still, it was the mask that could make anyone fierce.

"What do you want?" my mother asked the man.

"Master Entralgo wants the other woman."

Mother looked at Grandmother, wondering what she'd done wrong again. Grandmother sat on her hammock weaving, looking nonchalant, then she looked up.

"What does he want?" she inquired, not of him, but of Mother.

"You must come," the man told her.

Grandmother shrugged. "I've done nothing," she said. Then she got up from her hammock. "Almeydita, I want you to come with me and carry my basket."

I picked up her basket which had various medicines in it, as if it contained treasures.

"He didn't send for Almeydita," said my mother.

"No, he didn't send for the little one," said the man.

"What little one?" I pouted. I straightened my shoulders and placed my hands on my hips. Could this be Pao Joaquim? You don't defy Pao Joaquim.

"But I want her to come with me."

"All right. Do what you will. You'll do it anyway."

I walked behind my grandmother and the tall man, carrying the basket of charms and potions. When we reached the casa grande, we were taken into the music and sitting room. Entralgo was surrounded by all kinds of musical instruments and paintings. Indeed, I hadn't noticed Entralgo at first. But he had hung a hammock up and was lying in that and eating a mandacaru.

"Why've you brought that little girl?" he asked with anger.

He looked as if he were ready to swoop down on me. Did I remind him of Selvagem?

"She won't understand what language we speak in," retorted Grandmother. "Or why you've sent for me."

"Then tell me why I've sent for you, Old Witch?" he asked, throwing the mandacaru onto the carpeted floor. A servant whom I hadn't noticed came and scooped it up and put it in a basket. He waved the servant out and raised up somewhat to look at her out of hawk's eyes.

"For a gift I might give," she replied, looking at him steadily, and not from the corner of her eyes.

"There's no gift that such a woman as you might give to such a man as me."

"So you have no need of me," she said, turning.

"What did you bring?" he asked, motioning toward the basket.

"Do you think I can touch the eye and heal it without medicines?"

"What eye?"

"I thought it was the eye that needed to be healed. Isn't it the eye that's somewhat bloodshot?"

"No, it's not the eye," he said. "I've heard that men go to you for such problems, though, and though you're not exclusively concerned, not wholly concerned with such matters, you've been very helpful and have cured such problems. And that many times after you've healed the eye it gives no more trouble. It works as it should."

I looked at him, wondering why he was now talking about the eye when he had just said it was not the eye. And he looked like he had two good eyes.

"Yes, that's true, yes," she said. "I recommend coffee mixed with clots of menstrual blood of the desired woman, very strong coffee, and much sugar. Some say it's the blood of a mulatto woman that's the best, but I don't agree."

He sat looking at her with his mouth slightly open. "Do you want to poison me?"

"If you have trouble getting the menstrual blood, the other remedy I'd recommend is fresh air, plenty of exercise, not the kind you get beating Antonia...."

"Careful, Witch."

"....a change of food, plenty of vegetables and fruits. But besides that, Sir, I don't know what to recommend. As far as magic goes, Sir, I'm not very skilled."

"And not at all crazy either, I wager. Send the girl out."

"Sir, I'm not one of those magicians who can simply touch the eye and heal it."

He tossed his hand into the air and told my grandmother to get out, although after that one began to see him walk more and ride around less in his hammock, carried by servants. And I recall that Antonia began to be beaten not so frequently as before.

"What did that devil want?" my mother asked when we got back inside.

"Me to teach him how to be the master."

"What? What craziness is that? I've never seen more master. Has Antonia seen more master than that one?"

"To teach him to conquer himself," said grandmother, going back to her weaving. "To teach him to master himself."

Mother shook her head. "I don't know what you mean."

"He believes I have some sexual magic, but I told him I hadn't any." My grandmother gave a deep laugh.

Mother, silent, looked at me then at her. "He wanted you to cure him?" She looked at me again.

"No bad blood," my grandmother said. "A lack of power."

My mother gave a sigh of relief. I didn't know what it was about then, but learned later that the superstition was that only virgins could cure bad blood, and only black ones, though myth had it that there were very few of those.

My mother nodded, but still kept looking at me.

"She stayed outside," Grandmother said, although she did not explain that it was only in understanding that I'd been outside.

Gold

"What're you selling, Sir?" my grandmother asked the itinerant peddler, whom we met as we walked along the road gathering cashew nuts.

"Wigs, silk stockings, wine, olive oil, and wheaten flour."

"Wheaten flour?"

"Yes, and tobacco, brandy, rum."

"I'd like some wheaten flour."

The man, who was wearing high boots and a broad-brimmed hat, didn't move to get her any of the wheaten flour that was in the cart that he pulled along behind him. Finally, she reached into a hidden pocket in her skirt, took out a little bag and sprinkled bits of gold powder into her hand. When he saw it, his eyes lit up and he jumped down from his horse and went quickly to the side of the cart, and got a bag of wheaten flour. He opened a bag that he carried at his waist, and she emptied the gold powder into it.

"You see me today but you won't see me tomorrow," said the man.

"And why's that?" asked grandmother, holding the bag of wheaten flour in her fist.

"Cause I'm on my way to the gold mines at Minas Gerais. If I don't find gold I'll still be a rich man."

"How will you be a rich man if you don't find gold?" I asked. "How's that?"

"Cause he'll charge outrageous prices," said my grandmother. "Isn't that so, Sir?"

"Sim, I'll charge outrageous prices," he said with a laugh, going his way.

"Where'd you get the gold?" I asked as we walked back to the senzala.

She explained that when she'd gone into the interior of the country with Rugendas, into the sertao, they'd met Indians who lived in cities, not like the tiny mission villages along the coast, but real cities, and these Indians made many things out of gold, except that gold meant nothing to them.

"Were they Tupi?"

"No, the Tupis live near the coast. I don't know what names they have in the interior. Gold didn't mean a thing to them, though. They saw the tools that Rugendas carried, and exchanged their gold for his tools. Gold didn't mean a thing at all to them."

I asked her why she'd spent some of it on wheaten flour.

"It's enough for wheaten flour," she said, "but not enough to buy freedom. Did Rugendas have to buy his?"

A Conversation with Antonia

"Wait a minute, little girl," she called. "Come here, menina."

It was a Sunday and a holiday and she was sitting out in front of her hut, drinking rum. I'd been walking along the road as I always did on holidays. I'd gone to the palm grove where my grandmother had taken me. I'd still discovered no mysteries there nor had I seen the invisible Rugendas. I was on my way back to my mother's hut.

"Come over here, menina," she called again.

I went over and stood in front of her. She was a tall and big woman but not a fat one. She wore one of her breasts covered but the other free. A hard-drinking and hard-working woman she took no nonsense from anyone, and I wondered why she took it even from the master. Although she was a slave and he was the master, she still seemed to me, even then, a better woman than he was a man. She took a gulp of rum and stared at me in silence. Her eyes were bloodshot but sparkling.

"I'd like to invite you into my hut to talk to me," she said.

I shook my head and backed away from her.

"I like you, menina," she said. "Hasn't your spirit ever been attracted to someone?"

I nodded, though I only guessed at what she meant. She stood up and I followed her inside. She took her clay jug of rum with her. Her hut was very small with only one short hammock which looked as if she couldn't stretch out fully in it, many multi-colored mats that she'd woven from pieces of Sea Island cotton, clay jugs along the wall, some decorated with pretty designs. She motioned for me to sit down on one of the mats, while she sat on another one. She lifted the clay jug and took a swig of rum.

"Sim, who knows why the spirit attaches itself to someone," she said. "It's just the way and you don't know why." She took another swig of rum. "What do you think of my face? Do you think it's ugly or beautiful? Or can you tell?"

Another one for the negro asylum, I was thinking, as I watched her. She didn't frighten me, but I stood as far away from her as one could in that tiny hut. It was true she had one of those faces that could be different things for different people. Was she ugly or beautiful? It was difficult to tell. Her most generous features were her ears, which stuck out from puffs of fluffy black hair. The rest of her was cat-like, a small nose and mouth, slit-like but attractive eyes. And there were little marks on her face, like scratches, patterns that I'd mostly seen on the faces of old people and newly arrived Africans.

She gave a little laugh, as she looked at me.

"What d'you think of me? Do you like me?"

"Sim."

"He thinks I'm in the hands of the devil, that Entralgo. He thinks I've bewitched him," she said. She tilted her head to the side and gave a short jerk. My eyes widened. "That's why he sent for the Old Witch....That's what he calls her, not me."

I stood against the wall of the hut.

"You don't know whether I'm ugly or beautiful?" she asked

I shook my head no.

"And don't you know whether I'm good or evil either?"

"They say that you're a thief and a drunkard."

"Oh, do they? Yes, they do, don't they? So am I good or evil?"

I said that I couldn't decide.

"Well, after you have decided that, you must decide what punishment or what reward you'll give me."

"How can I reward or punish you?" I asked. I felt like the little one the tall servant had called me.

She looked at me for a long moment.

"No, I'm not beautiful," she said suddenly. "And I'm not ugly either."

She drank another swig from her rum, then she gave me a look like Entralgo had Selvagem when I thought he would swoop down on her. Then she wiped her right hand across her mouth, then up and down her right thigh. Her thigh had scars and scratches on it too. Her eyes seemed to grow smaller as she looked at me.

"D'you think I'd bewitch a man?" she asked. "D'you think I could do it? I'm not very beautiful. But he thinks I bewitched him and so he got your grandmother to unbewitch him….Do you think the master takes care of me?"

I asked her didn't he take care of all of us, since he owned us.

"Owns us, eh? We're in a foreign land, menina. It's not our own. We're in a foreign land that's not our own. What land d'you live in?"

"The same as you."

She clucked. "Why my spirit's attracted to you, I don't know. But you won't be able to forget about me, either. He thinks I've enchanted him and so he got your grandmother to disenchant him. It's she wanted me to tell you that, as if she couldn't tell you well enough her own self." She swallowed more rum. "I'm a generous woman and I'm not wicked. I'm only unmanageable. There are things I won't swallow. Things I won't swallow, you see. No, not a bit. I've got no magic charms."

She arched her back.

"I heal fast, only because of the help of your grandmother, but me I have no magic charms. I'm just an ordinary mulher, not wicked. There are just things I won't swallow." She leaned toward me and I backed into the wall. If I could have become the wall, I would have.

"See that woman?"

I peeked out her door. It was Mexia there in the road. Yes, I nodded that I saw her.

"Her eyes are as meek as a cow's, as meek as a cow's. Do you know what relationship there's between her and the old priest?"

"Sim," I said meekly.

"Is she good or evil?"

I tried to remember Father Tollinare's question.

"Yes, you know it, but you won't say."

I tried to remember how Father Tollinare had phrased it.

"She's got some power over the old priest or he's got some power over her. But she's a fool and a simpleton. Nobody should be as yielding and pliable as that."

I felt as if she were talking about a different woman, not the Mexia that I knew, but I nodded anyway.

"She doesn't know she's in a foreign country that's not her own. She thinks it's hers too. They call me a drunkard and a thief, but I'm not so drunk as that, and I can't steal a land that's not my own."

She took a new swig of rum, swirled it in her mouth, and swallowed. She put her hand to her lips and belched, without excusing herself. "I don't know why, but the spirit's a funny thing. Mine's very jolly when I see you. Do you know why everybody calls me a drunkard and a thief?"

"No."

"Because he started it. Entralgo. He started it so everyone took it up, whether they knew it to be true or not. I drink yes because I'm in a foreign land that's not my own."

I stared at the scratches on her thigh.

"But I've stolen nothing," she continued. "Now he's got two new names for me. Now he calls me a madwoman and a murderer, but I dare him to spread that about. I dare him to." She slapped her hand across her thigh.

We looked at each other for a long time. She arched her back again, then she came forward and caressed me, and said again that she didn't know what moved one spirit toward another.

"My grandmother told me to tell you all this. I wouldn't have otherwise. Of my own nature, I don't speak such things."

Then she apologized for keeping me too long, although I felt I could have stayed longer then. "May God keep you," she whispered, then took her eternal swig of rum.

Dr. Johann

"Acaiba, bring Almeydita."

My mother brought me outside. I stared at the green hills but not at the white man who was standing in front of us.

"Is this the one?" Entralgo asked him.

The stranger was a young man, about twenty, although he seemed older to me then. I stared at the green hills and then at the man from the corner of my eyes. He had high cheekbones and full lips, his dark eyes slanted downwards. I looked at him fully. He was more beautiful than handsome and there was something womanly about him.

"Yes," he nodded, looking at me. He wasn't really smiling, but he looked at me in a full way that made me feel he was not from this country. Now I might describe his look as a mixture of curiosity and tenderness. Still I'm not sure. It was one of those kinds of looks that changes meaning with time and place. Certainly, he was not from this country.

"Dr. Johann wants to paint her," Entralgo said to my mother. "Bring her to the veranda."

We went onto the veranda and then followed them into the place with thick white walls and oriental carpets and Dutch chandeliers. I was taken into the interior of the house, the part of the house where the doctor was staying, toward the back, a room with Dutch windows facing the orchard. Most of the house was dark and damp and I was glad for the sunshine.

"Do you want the other wench to stay?" asked Entralgo.

Dr. Johann looked at my mother. He gave her a different look. "Yes," he said. "I might want to include her too."

I'd never seen a man like him before. A master would give you a bold look but not a full one. I assume now that it was because not simply that he was not from this country, but that he was an artist. He explained to my mother and me--he spoke to us directly--that he had seen me in the yard and that my face had interested him, particularly the huge eyes--he called them "dark, intelligent" eyes, not the sort of eyes that you'd describe a slave as having, and he had wanted to paint me. But he added that I had a miserable body, so skinny. Entralgo interrupted to say that I was fed well and lazy enough--"All of them are lazy enough," he added, meaning both my mother and grandmother too. He said that we were all useless as field hands and more haughty for our own good so he'd set us to weaving baskets and making hammocks and such. "But a more well fed or lazier bunch you'll never see," he said.

Dr. Johann didn't reply to his harangue, he simply told me where to stand to get the best of the light, while he stood behind a long board, a canvas I learned, and held a brush and a smaller board full of an assortment of many different colors. He told my mother who stood back watching me that she might stand closer near me. Entralgo stood by looking serious, then bewildered and curious, then disgusted.

"But, Senhor, there are so many white women in the house," said Entralgo.

"I have seen so many white women," replied Dr. Johann. He put on a bored expression.

Entralgo stood by watching, then grunted and left. Every now and then as he worked, Dr. Johann would come to me and touch my hair and run his hands along my jaw and touch the lids of my eyes. His hands were soft and I found myself waiting for him to stop painting and come and touch me. My mother stood in silence and watched him with some wariness until he finished that day and then the next day and the next I was taken there, while my mother would stand waiting. Then one day it was not me that Dr.Johann wanted but my mother.

"Leave Almeydita here," Entralgo's messenger said when he came to our hut. "Dr. Johann wants you alone today."

"Almeydita can watch as he paints me," my mother hastened to say.

"He wants you alone," repeated the messenger, looking at her sternly.

Mother left with him. When she returned she was very silent.

"Did you see the painting of me?" I asked with excitement. "Has he finished mine?"

She stared at me, then she said "He wanted your face and eyes, but my body."

Her solemn face had made mine turn solemn.

"Will he paint you tomorrow?" I asked.

"Yes," she said. Then she knelt in the corner of the hut, lifting rice in her hands.

I pictured Dr. Johann coming to her and touching her as he'd done me, her jawline and her eyelids. She was silent, standing stiffly and solemn. I wanted to ask something, but she was too silent, and she wouldn't look at me. I watched her preparing the rice. I peeked out the door of the hut and saw Dr. Johann sitting on a rock painting a man who was standing holding a basket and a woman who was balancing a basket of bananas on her head. I tried to imagine the painting he'd done--with the face and eyes of a young girl and the body of a woman. Dr. Johann looked over his canvas. I half-imagined that he saw me, but his eyes returned to his canvas. I pulled back inside and my mother handed me a plate of coconut and rice and onions.

Tempo, the horse trader

He was a man who kept horses, not for white men but for himself. He lived outside of the plantation in a square hut made of mud bricks and straw. Whenever I'd go with my mother to the stream with the other women, I could catch glimpses of Tempo on the side of the hill with his five saddle horses, or four or three, that he rented out to people, or exchanged with men who were traveling distances on the road and needed fresh horses. Because he wasn't a branco, he couldn't ride them his own self, although he was free. At the stream, I'd kneel with my mother, rinsing clothes after she'd washed them, wringing them and putting them into a basket. I'd beg my mother if I could race up to the hillside and see him.

"See who?" she'd always ask, although she knew who I meant.

"Senhor Tempo, Senhor Tempo," I'd say impatiently.

"Go ahead," she'd say with a slight smile.

I'd rush up to the hillside and he'd be waiting for me and smiling. Always he wore a loose gray-white shirt and gray-white trousers and carried a pole or stick. He'd help me up on one of the horses, and he'd hold the bridle and we'd walk around the small barn where he slept in straw alongside the horses. Because I was a menina, he thought he could bend the laws for me.

"How old are you now, Almeydita?" he'd ask, although I kept telling him the same thing, or it seemed like I always told him the same thing. He knew perfectly well my age.

"I'm eight," I'd say, stroking the horse's mane. Once it had been seven, once six, once five that I'd said, but it was always the same question.

Then he'd be silent and we'd walk around and around the barn until my mother lifted her arm and waved. Then he'd help me off the horse, holding me by my thin waist.

My mother had never come up there with me and had never that I could remember spoken to the man, yet whenever I would leave he'd say, "Give Acaiba my best thoughts."

I'd smile and he'd nod at me and I'd rush down the hill to the women gathering up laundry. Then we'd go to another place and I'd help my mother hang the wet clothes on bushes and low trees. If I'd been older I might have noticed a certain look my mother had whenever I'd return from Tempo. She'd be silent but there'd be that certain look, and once when we returned to our hut she spoke aloud.

"He's the only free man I know," she said. She was silent, then she said, "Or maybe he just thinks he's a free man. Maybe he just thinks he's free."

A Man Comes to Ride a Horse and Work on a Dictionary

After Dr. Johann arrived, my mother was brought to work in the household, in the casa grande. I was many times there working along with her and so got to see many visitors. Since there were no inns in our part of the country--and indeed in most of Brazil there were no inns--those with letters of introduction and visiting dignitaries were allowed to stay at the casa grande; those without letters of introduction, if they were not thieves or ruffians were allowed to camp on the outskirts of the plantation or in the fields surrounding the senzala. Therefore many of the visitors were not even relatives of Entralgo, but having letters of introduction from noblemen and viceroys and other senhores de engenho, a caudilho or coronel, fazendeiro, or ouvidor--more were welcome as if they were, as plantation owners did in those days, and were given guest rooms. Rubber gatherers, cowboys, muleteers, slave-hunters, bushwhacking captains, tropas de resgate and the like had to camp on the outskirts of the plantation or near the senzala.

Well, this one senhor was a short, dark-haired man with blue steel eyes. When we first saw him, everyone was told to come out into the yard and even the family of Entralgo was brought out sitting in hammocks, except the women and the girls of course were in covered hammocks.

Immediately the visitor jumped onto one of the horses and began to ride. Grinning like a lunatic, he stood up on the horse's back as it galloped at full speed. Then stepping down as if he were falling, but holding onto the horn, he pulled himself up again. Next he jumped from one side of the horse to the other, climbed under its belly to the other side, disappeared several times behind the horse and appeared again. He did other stunts and acrobatics. His expressions brought laughter, his tricks delight. My grandmother had once told me that her mapmaker, Rugendas, was capable of such stunts.

When he jumped down from the horse, everyone applauded, the master most raucously. I went with my mother to prepare the meal. After dinner I was told to bring the visitor water, a glass of strong beer and a Portuguese cigar. He was sitting at a mahogany writing table bending over some papers. I was surprised to find a man doing such stunts bending over papers. He didn't look like a simple licenciado. Most scholars had squinty eyes, and his, though they squinted some to look at the papers, flashed clear and generous when they looked at me. He wasn't exactly a polished man either, but he wasn't as coarse as a muleteer. He motioned for me to set the water, beer, and cigar on the table. His look was cantankerous.

"I tell him that a dictionary of the Brazilian language should not be only academic Portuguese words, but should include Indian words and contributions to the language by Negroes and others."

I look at him. I'd never heard a branco speak to me in such a way, not even Dr. Johann. When he noticed I didn't understand him, he explained.

"Father Tollinare and I, you see, are working on a Brazilian dictionary. He feels I'm making it imperfect by the impure words I wish to put into it. So we finished it in the strictest most unadulterated Portuguese, but now I'm doing my own supplement, you see. Now I'm collecting as many of the 'impure' words and phrases as are common only to this New World. When one is in a new world one must have new words, you see. Certainly the contributions of the first Brazilians should be here, at least the first ones that we know about, and what the Negroes brought here along with the Portuguese. You see what I'm saying? Why are you looking at me so? Do you think I'm a funny man?"

I shook my head.

"Do I look like a man of learning, then?"

I shook my head again.

He said he was a self-taught man and he mentioned places he had traveled to, places in New Spain, and in the Old World too--Paris and London. I wondered if self-taught meant that he was a man of as much learning as Father Tollinare. I wondered whether he had read forbidden books.

"Did you like my riding this morning?"

"Sim."

"Well, you've seen the only two things that I'm good at, putting together dictionaries and doing stunt rides. Well, in New Spain I'm good at *juego de canas*. Do you know what that is?"

"No."

"Jousting, my dear. It's done on horseback and it's like throwing javelins, except it's done for sport at holiday and we only use lightweight canes."

"Are you from New Spain?"

"No, I was born and bred right here." He gulped his strong beer, lit the Portuguese cigar and took a few puffs. "I don't know anything else. Oh, I know a thing or two about the world and a thing or two about the imagination, but it's not stuff you can use really except in a book or two. I'm a very timid man."

"You don't act timid."

"Sim. Dictionaries and stunt riding. I do one thing because I do the other. I balance my timidity with a show of recklessness, but it's all very controlled, every bit of it. I'm not at all spontaneous really. Long, patient, difficult work. And that's from a well-traveled man but a man who also has a disposition for leisure, strong beer, and a good cigar." He nodded, smoked, took another huge swallow of beer. "If it were up to me, perhaps, I wouldn't be so well-traveled. My father, now that's a lover of adventure and novelties. It's he taught me to stunt ride while my mother wanted me to be a licenciado at some great University in Europe. My father's an archeologist. He's somewhere in Africa or India now and my mother's traipsing with him. Me, I came back here because I wanted to make something of the New World. So I say this is important work. Do you think dictionary-making is important work?"

I said I didn't know. I wondered whether a dictionary could include forbidden words, but I didn't ask him.

"Is it important? Well, I make claims that it is. You use a word, but me I isolate, analyze, explain, give history to. My father thinks it's some silliness I've gotten myself into, some estupidez, some obsession. Even Father Tollinare and I have disputes on what are the highest and most imaginative words. I say one thing and he says the other, and he wants to ban some words altogether; he doesn't want those in the Old World to see the new one as a prurient or vulgar place. But if the words are here, I say use them. He says one thing and I say another. I say one thing and he says another. It's not just imagination that's meaningful in a word, it's the preservation of tradition. That's the important thing. The purpose of a dictionary, he says, is not to say what words are in use, but what words should be in use. He'd transport the whole Portuguese language here, if he could, not taking into account what changes would be naturally made, how one comes to terms linguistically with new geography and experiences. When I was in Portugal they laughed at the way I spoke my native language. Perhaps that's what obsessed me, and even Father Tollinare complains that I don't talk much like a lexicographer."

"What's a lexicographer?"

"Why, a compiler of dictionaries. That's what I am. Didn't I say so? I don't talk much like one, you see, and I don't have letters of credence from a University. And in Portugal they laughed at my native tongue, called it barbaric. So I'm making my own little supplement on the New World Poruguese. Do you hear what I'm saying? A maker of dictionaries. For my father, that doesn't begin to be anything for a man to do, a real man, a true man. He'd never understand. Do you think it's something for a man to do, even a man without letters of credence?"

I wasn't sure what letters of credence were. I said, however, I didn't know.

"A man should live within his own imagination. By that, I mean what he can imagine himself to be. How can he live beyond it?"

I kept looking at the man. His hair was so black it looked blue.

"Ah, this is a very useful expression," he said, scribbling something on the paper. "What if it doesn't mean literally what it says. Sometimes we use words here as we imagine them to mean."

He didn't tell me what the word was and I couldn't make out his scribbling. Perhaps it was a word I shouldn't know. Perhaps it was forbidden.

"All of this in just one word," he mumbled.

Since he had not dismissed me, I remained standing there.

"What is it you want?" he asked, looking at me suddenly, as if noticing I was still there, or noticing me for the first time.

"I'm waiting for you to dismiss me, Sir."

He looked at me, then looked down at his work again, then scribbled something else. Strangely, he still did not dismiss me. He gulped some more beer and puffed again.

"How many hyphens?" he asked himself. "I could write volumes and volumes of supplements, but Father Tollinare despises this, he ridicules it. But this is a new country. Who knows which language will develop here. Especially fertile is the linguistic imagination of the lower classes. And all kinds of words have entered our language from the Guinea coast."

"Guinea coast?"

"Don't you know your own country?"

"I know a Guinea fowl when I see one."

"Our native expressions....What was I saying?"

"The Guinea coast."

"All new countries have a murderous tongue, but that's how one survives. That's a New world. Who knows what Father Tollinare despises now might be what someday distinguishes our whole country. And if your people had their way, little black girl...." He looked at me, but didn't continue what he was going to say. "I've heard free negroes talk, the learned ones, the ones with pretensions and they're worse than Father Tollinare."

"Father Tollinare's from Portugal."

"He claims that, does he? He's a Mazombo like the rest of us."

"Macumba?"

"A Brazilian born in the New World not the Old. Of European parents of course. Macumba is the Guinea version of our Holy Faith. Father Tollinare….this has nothing to do with religion."

"How can a priest have nothing to do with religion?"

He looked impatient, cantankerous again. "What I'm saying though about the Guineas who try to use a privileged language, like the criollos, their language is the most circumscribed, the most absolutely perfect, rigid, unimaginative guff. All they've learned well is the language of the Master…."

"But you just said they were free."

"Some are free, others merely pretentious. The language that prevents subversiveness is what I'm saying, just like the criollos and there's talk among some criollos of one day having our own country where we can make our own cigars and don't have to always import expensive Portuguese ones. Do you know that we can't even make our own cigars in our own country? No manufactured things, only raw materials. That's what a colony means. They talk of winning our freedom, but shouldn't we be free to use our own language?"

"What does a colony mean?"

"That you must import every manufactured thing. Didn't you know that? But you have never been to the coast. Raw goods go out and manufactured goods come in. It is the same in New Spain. It's a crime to even manufacture our own rum."

"Antonia makes her own."

"Antonia? Eh, some slave girl. Antonia? I've heard that name. The rascal, he calls her. Why, this is a world of rascals. These are the laws of import-export I'm talking about. It's all economics and the official prohibition of anything manufactured here, even the moustache cup. Shall you deny me my moustache cup?"

"No," I said and started to rush about to find one.

"Come back here."

I came and stood before him again. He squinted his eyes at me.

"You don't look dumb," he said. "You look well-fed. You look like one who always drinks the beastings. Language, let me tell you, has its own genius for rebellion or compromise. And should we always import our art from Europe, as Entralgo does even his paintings?"

I started to tell him of Dr. Johann, but he was so rapid with his talk that I just listened.

"My father goes hunting for lost races and the races are here!" he shouted. "Try to improve the ones here and now I say and he calls me a discredit to the family. He's off to some magic desert and I'm here where the manioc grows. So, you see I'm a maker of dictionaries and a clown and acrobat. Do you think I'm a clown? Do you think I'm uncultivated?"

"Sim," I answered, although I was uncertain what he meant.

"Well, this is a land of clowns, or at least exaggerated personalities. But isn't this a country enough for that? Don't we have passion enough for that? Just like you drink the beastings. Anyway, we should all take advantage of opportunities for racial improvement, shouldn't we? When I was in Europe, I married a Swiss prostitute. How's that for improving the race? I tried studying archeology, but I changed to etymology. The spoils of my father's adventures all go to museums. And my mother traipses about with him, like a woman on the edge of a storm. This dictionary-making, child, this is patient, difficult work." He took another swig of beer. "Antonia, did you say? Well, Entralgo and his slave-making activities. Me, I'm a lover of language. New words for a new landscape, that's what I say. Authority and submission. Subject and object. I see you're an intelligent little girl. This word here is from the Dutch. Eh, this is a common error. And this an uncommon one. Words for a new generation. Keep the secret. Can you keep a secret?" He took another swig of beer and leaned into my ear. "Language and politics, my child, is very interesting." He leaned back into his papers. "Let us return now to the previous footnote. Very interesting. Similar in style these two personal expressions. This letter. What do you think?"

"I don't know."

Just then Father Tollinare came into the room, saw the young man had gotten quite drunk, and motioned for me to leave. When I was outside I heard him say, "Foolish boy" and "Foolish notion" and "but a language of tremendous prestige" and "off with our boots."

And I heard the young man reply, "But, Padre, you hyperbolize, you hypercriticize, you hyperbola, he he, you hyperborean, you hypercatalectic hyperborean, you hyperesthetic hypercatalectic hyperborean, you must confront the realities of life, the realities of language. The beastings?"

"Foolish boy," I heard Father Tollinare say.

I did not hear anything else for my mother came, saw me eavesdropping and drew me away.

The Woman and Palmares

I'd never seen a black woman dressed like her before. She rode up in a carriage beside a white man. People along the road stopped and gaped at her. Those inside came to the doors of their huts. She was dressed in a long silk gown full of pleats and folds and ruffles and there was a crucifix around her neck. Her hair was straightened and tied in a ball just like a branca's. Her neck looked very thick and deformed, but my mother explained to me that that was the kind of woolen collar that she wore in the city. It was considered very stylish, very much in vogue, although she agreed with me that it did look like some deformity, and must be very hot in this climate, but near the coast it was not so hot as here, though hot enough.

The crucifix sat between the woman's breasts. The woman herself sat very straight and tall. I looked at her feet, though, and saw that she was wearing no shoes. She was as barefoot as myself, and her toes stuck out from the full pleats. I smiled. I saw other people smiling too but I felt it was for a different reason. I myself was in awe of her. I can't describe the white man very well, because it was the woman who kept my attention. However, I remember that he was wearing a broad hat and a dark suit. The woman's eyes were slanted upward and there was a gold comb in her hair, like a little crown. She seemed extraordinarily tall, but perhaps it was where she was riding, right in the front seat beside the man.

"Who's that woman?" I whispered to my mother.

I've not described my mother. A big-boned, handsome woman, she did not comb her hair down or tie it in scarves like some of the other women; she wore it so that it looked like the crown of a tree, high all around her head. She said nothing until she went and got her long pipe that was in the corner of the room. A long slender reed, the stem pointed downward and ended below her knees, then there was a very small bowl. I didn't know what she smoked in it, as I'd smelled tobacco and it wasn't that.

"I don't know. I've heard stories of her, though," she replied.

"What stories?"

She looked at me without speaking and drew at her pipe. She looked as if she were thinking through something, which she didn't tell me, then she said "Some say she's a princess from Africa…."

"From Guinea coast?" I asked, my eyes wide.

"From Africa," she repeated, "and that that white man, that branco, went and got her and brought her here and shared his wealth with her." She puffed on her pipe, then added snidely, "Or she shared hers with him."

And there was something else. This she thought though, but didn't say.

"Why were they laughing at her?" I asked.

"Cause he's dressed her up to look like a white woman, a branca, eh, that's why they laugh. Cause of the way he's dressed her up."

"If I wore a silk dress would they laugh at me too?"

"Where'd you get a silk dress?" she asked. "Or brocades or satin or velvet too. You do good to get Sea Island cotton. Or muslin too."

I said nothing. She took a draw from her long pipe.

"I bet she's got diamonds and gold rings. I bet she's got a velvet saddle and diamond sevigne too."

"What d'you know of diamond sevigne?" she asked, and drew on her long pipe. "Straw sapatos do you good."

My mother and I were the ones who were sent for to come up to the casa grande to see about the new guests. I didn't know how to treat the woman except as a branca. She was sitting in a big chair in the room they'd given her. When I came in with the angel cakes I was to bring to her, she wouldn't look at me. She held her head high, but wouldn't look even in my direction. They'd given her an elegant room with Dutch furniture, but the women of the house didn't gather around her as they did when other lady guests arrived. Then the women of the house would go off into the mistress' room and gather around the new lady, sitting on pillows and mats or lying in hammocks, chewing plums or sweet cakes. But this lady sat alone and very straight in a wooden chair with her bare feet sticking out from the hem of her dress. She wouldn't look at me and there was nothing I could say to her. I thought of the slave women gathering around her and of Antonia offering her a swig of rum and my mother a puff from her long pipe. And I'd bring her a mandacaru. But I felt that it would be somehow wrong and that she wouldn't like it. I set the tray of angel cakes down on her table and bowed to her. I curtsied properly like to any lady. She held her back like an arrow.

"Are you a slave woman or a free woman?" I dared to ask.

"I am neither kind," she answered, still without looking at me.

In the living room, the men, my mother related to me, spoke of Palmares for the benefit of Dr. Johann, who had heard stories and legends of the settlements of escaped slaves and had asked Entralgo and the other senhores native to the region to speak of it. He had wished, he said, to travel where they were and to paint them, but both the visitor and Entralgo and the other senhores present persuaded him or rather dissuaded him, saying that it was foolish, it would be too dangerous. They'd cut off his ears and feet. And they spoke also of how the Palmaristas, as these fugitive devils were called--that was their language--had had some women stolen some years ago, some comely women. No, not white women, gracas a Deus, but black ones and Indians. But stealing white women wasn't beyond those devils. That time, though, they hadn't. The savages had killed no one, that time, they'd only taken from the stores and stolen the women, but that was a long time ago, because with the aid of the Paulistas, they'd driven them further into the forests and mountains, so that kind of thing they didn't expect. Some comely women too, repeated Entralgo. He himself was just a boy, but he could appreciate....But it would be dangerous and foolish, he told the senhor, even if he did want to keep an artistic record of the times, hadn't he gotten enough black faces already? Anyway, what he'd like to know, pelo amor de Deus, where were his white sketches of the New World? Was it only those people he wanted to depict for immortality? What did he have to show to the estrangeiros of the lovely white senhoras e senhorinhas and the interesting white senhores of the territory? All the possibilities and challenges to his talent were right there. He couldn't understand himself how Dr. Johann could see any interest or complexities in those pretos. For complexity or interest a branco or a branca anyday. Why didn't he paint pictures of the people in whom man's fate lay? Wouldn't that be a challenge to his artistic talents? These others, these pretos, they'd forever be a threat to Brazilian progress and civilization. He could tell Dr. Johann was after all an artist of intellect and religious feeling.

"There're enough black faces around here already," Entralgo had said. "What, to paint new ones. No, Senhor, you don't have to put yourself in the way of danger to get any more of them. And like I said aren't there lovely and interesting white people in this territory, who'd challenge your talents more?"

"Sim, sim, sim, sim," toasted some of the senhores present.

"The captain could direct me how to get them," said Dr. Johann. "I know it wouldn't be an easy thing."

Entralgo laughed and continued laughing. The captain said nothing.

"Even the captain has fought his last expedition against the negroes. But with him it's an example of what love can do. Captain Goncalo has discovered that even negroes are human."

Captain Goncalo was silent. He sat stiffly in a chair. Entalgo lay in a hammock. Dr. Johann sat with his arm thrown along the back of a couch.

"My wife lived in Palmares for four years," Captain Goncalo told Dr. Johann. "She was one of the captured women."

"You do not kill them in these wars?"

Entralgo laughed hard, causing his hammock to swing. My mother stood near fanning him and handing him imported chocolates and bits of angel cake. Dr. Johann, she said, looked at her every now and then as if she were doing something disrespectful, not for herself, but to him. She said "him" but I did not know whether she meant Dr. Johann himself or Entralgo.

"Few women are ever killed. Those negroes who are captured are divided among the soldiers."

"And that one he could not resist," Entralgo said. "And in your love for her haven't you turned her into a laughing stock?"

Captain Goncalo was silent. He cleared his throat. He stood up. Dr. Johann looked at my mother.

"There'd be no guarantees for your safety if you were to go on an expedition against the negroes," said the Captain.

"It wouldn't be *against* them," said Dr. Johann.

"And who knows perhaps a little negrita would be distributed to you if you were to escape with your life," Entralgo said.

He opened his mouth and my mother popped a chocolate inside. Dr. Johann gave her that look.

"I'd really like very much to go," he said then. "There's some more work I'd like to finish up here, and then I'd like it if you'd write me a letter of introduction to someone."

"Letters of introduction to negroes?" asked Entralgo. "Is this the new world?"

"I don't mean that," explained Dr. Johann. "I mean to another captain when they go on their next expedition."

Captain Goncalo nodded and was silent. My mother felt that he was thinking about the woman even before he spoke.

"My wife tried to commit suicide twice when she was first with me." He paused, looking at no one. "She's not tried to commit suicide now in a number of years."

"What? Her desire for liberty isn't so great now, eh?" Entralgo said and laughed. "Scratch my head," he told my mother.

My mother scratched his head and picked a lice from it. Captain Goncalo was silent. Dr. Johann stared at my mother. She parted Entralgo's hair, searched and searched for more lice.

"I took her back," Captain Goncalo said. "After the second time she tried to kill herself, we went back there only to find Palmares had been abandoned. They'd left that part and gone somewhere else and formed a new Palmares, those who were not killed or captured. 'Do we continue our journey?' I asked. She'd simply sat down and began to cry. 'Do we continue our journey?' I asked again. 'Sim,' she said, but it was back the way we had come that she pointed. It was then that I kept her for my wife. I took her legally for my wife."

"He He," laughed Entralgo. "Is that a lie or a true story?"

"Weren't you afraid to go back there alone with one of their women? Suppose they'd been there?"

"They say the leader has a blonde wench," Entralgo said. "One of his women's a blonde wench. But perhaps she has some Guinea ancestor. I've an imaginary Guinea ancestor. Ha. Ha. Don't we all? Everybody in this country has an imaginary Guinea. No No. I can prove I'm of good blood and purely European. I'm of pure blood."

"I always imagine that's what the woman was thinking," Captain Goncalo said in reply to Dr. Johann. "I had taken her back there anyway, regardless of what harm might be done. I imagine that's why she came back with me."

"It's not true, Captain, I can't believe it, it's not true," Entralgo said, pushing my mother's fingers out of his hair. "What's your true feeling for the woman? Dr. Johann, go and paint the wench for him. Go and paint the wench for him to see what she's really like. Show him what she's really like. Use your talent, man. Go and paint the wench for him. That's what you can do for this territory, show us what the devils are really like."

"Sir," Captain Goncalo said to Dr. Johann. "I'm going to my room and to my wife now. I'll write you a brief introduction to a Captain Moreira who'll be leading an expedition against the negroes very soon now, and perhaps you'll be able to accompany him. But for your own safety, Sir, I would agree with Senhor Entralgo, that you should remain in this territory, as the blacks are not very dangerous here."

"Not dangerous," Entralgo said with a grunt. "Rascals every one of them."

"Not very dangerous," continued the captain, "and you'll be able to collect a number of excellent faces...."

"But not nearly so interesting and complex...."

"A number of very excellent types even among the negroes here and the various Indian tribes, the Tupi, the...."

"That's an idea for you," Entralgo said. "Have Father Tollinare take you to see the Indians. Do you think the Negroes are the only dark people here? Go see the Indians. It would be less dangerous and your safety would be better guaranteed. At least our Indians here are quiet....except for the men, they're always running off. Except they are such loners in the forests. They're such mavericks."

"Yes, I'd appreciate a letter of introduction. I'll stay here a bit longer as I intended to visit the Indian groups," Dr. Johann said.

"Yes, Father Tollinare has them all in hand." Entralgo waved his hand in the air. "Except for the men, like I said, they're such mavericks. Living alone in the forests, the way some of them do."

My mother watched his hand in the air. She saw Dr. Johann observing her, disapprovingly, and so stared at nothing.

Captain Goncalo sat down at a huge desk, wrote a brief letter, folded it, and presented it to Dr. Johann.

"It's been a great pleasure to meet you," he said standing, bowing to Dr. Johann. Dr. Johann bowed and said it had been his pleasure to meet a man such as the Captain.

Captain Goncalo bowed to Entralgo and said "Sir I am no longer a guest in your house, nor will be from this day."

He stood stiffly and walked out.

Entralgo laughed and put my mother's hands back in his hair. Dr. Johann looked at them both, then he told Entralgo that he was going for a short walk.

"And then we'll dine," Entralgo said, still laughing. "But go see the Father, he'll be glad to show you where the Indians are. He knows them quite intimately." He chuckled. "My father had a number of them, but I prefer to do without them myself, but I have a number of the mixed variety, the caboclos. They provide some variety, you see. Some diversion for the eye."

A High Post in the Government

He was an intelligent, tall, and attractive young Indian. He'd been one of Father Tollinare's students many years before, and had been sent to study in Europe, first Paris and then Berlin. The older people knew of him. My mother said that she knew of him and that they were about the same age. In those days my mother was in her early twenties, though I don't know her exact age. She said that she too had been one of Father Tollinare's students, which surprised me, because she'd never given any indication that she knew either how to read or write. She explained that she'd been among the generation of "experiments." In those early days, she said, they believed that the Senegalese Negro with a drop of Arabic blood was the most intelligent, and so even though her mother was thought as "the crazy woman," Father Tollinare had chosen her anyway among other little girls. Still, whenever she saw me with my copybook she behaved around me shyly, as if what I was doing was something very strange.

"Your grandmother speaks and writes Arabic," she said now, as she watched Father Tollinare parading the ground with the dark-suited young man, whose Portuguese name was Alejandro but whose Tupi name my mother couldn't remember and confessed that perhaps he himself had forgotten it if he had ever known it as a boy. "But she would let none of *them* know. And me, she'd laugh at me when I'd read out of their books. She'd laugh and then recite long poems in Arabic. Odes, she'd call them. Qasidas. She'd sing of dark-eyed and dark-lipped people, just like us. And she'd make fun of Father Tollinare always having us pray a lot, always on our knees. She'd pound her own knees with laughter. Yet, I remember as a child she'd always pray a lot, on her own knees, and recite that strange language she refused to teach me. And *her* copybooks full of those strange scribblings; she keeps them hidden. Qasidas. I remember that though, like my own name. She'd eat sprigs of wild onion and sing of Amru al-Qays and Labid and Tarafah."

I said nothing. For some reason, I thought of the woman, Captain Goncalo's wife riding off in the wagon and looking haughty when they left Entralgo's plantation, looking as haughty as a branca. I imagined her with scrolls around her neck and waist instead of jewels. I imagined her hiding her scrolls in secret places, even keeping them from her husband, Captain Goncalo.

Alejandro was silent while Father Tollinare spoke loudly and with his hands. He seemed very proud of the young man and wanted to show him off. I felt eager to go for the lesson that day, thinking I'd catch a closer glimpse of the young man. And I did, for as I entered Father Tollinare had him sitting in the front of the room, in a cane chair up beside his desk. He never spoke, but I was sure that Father Tollinare had him sitting up there as an example to us. (Later I found out from Father Tollinare that the young man had asked him who I was, after I'd read my lesson, and although I'd only met him in his silence, it had made me very proud. He was one of those people, like Mexia's, whose presence remained with one.)

When class was dismissed, I left with the other children, but went back to the low window to peek at him again. He still sat stiffly, watching Father Tollinare, who made excited gestures. From that angle, in profile he reminded me of one of those still and silent Egypian pharaohs I'd seen in one of Dr. Johann's paintings. He said that it was a reproduction of a painting which he'd seen in one of the museums of Europe. I was so drawn to it that he gave it to me, but when Father Tollinare saw me with it he took it from me, declaring Egypt to be an evil world peopled by worshippers of serpents, and that the only paintings I should have were those of the Holy Virgin.

Peeking in at the low window, I could hear clearly what Father Tollinare was saying. He began to tell Alejandro that he had hopes for him with regard to a certain high post in the government. I knew that the brancos were becoming not opposed to having Indians in such high positions now, as in the early days when they considered Indians mere savages and children and though the majority of Indians were still thought mere savages and children, yet some of the brancos now, who referred to themselves as indianists, had even begun to boast of their Indian ancestors, even those with only imaginary ones. The Indian, I once remembered hearing Father Tollinare say, was what distinguished Brazil from the Old World.

Anyway, Father Tollinare began to tell him of a certain Indian, a captain-major who'd had such a grand position, and what had he done? Why, he'd done something unworthy of that honor. He'd been informed that he shouldn't, that under no circumstances, should he marry a certain preto woman, that he shouldn't tarnish his good blood with hers, but what had he done? Why, he'd done so anyway.

One priest had refused to marry them, but they'd found another who would. Some profligate. And so, the Indian, the captain-major had been dismissed from that high position in which he might have attained even greater honors.

Now that Alejandro knew that history, he said, he should not commit the same error.

"No, my boy, there are important men here who know of you, quite important men, who know of you and who have been anxious for your return. Yes, my boy."

Certainly, Father Tollinare explained, he'd first sent him to study abroad because he expected when he returned he would enter the priesthood, but now things were changing, there were more choices, more recognition of an Indian's humanity. And everyone had heard such magnificent accounts of him, his intelligence, his moral virtue.

He'd hoped that Alejandro would by now have forgotten the woman and his affection for her. He himself had seen that affection blossoming and that's partly why he'd sent him away. Even though she has the blood of the Indian, of his own people, there is Negro blood there too, and so she is all preto, or might as well be, and if he were to marry her, why, there'd be no place in the government, no worthy position for him, no position of honor.

He himself, he went on, recognized that she was a real and human woman.

"Yes, Alejandro, as I myself recognized that you are real and human. But I'm not a man of my own century, you see. Even so, I must look realistically at my own century. I must be pragmatic. Why, years ago, I'd have been that priest who'd have not refused to marry them. I'd have been that profligate. But now I'm a pragmatic man and I must look realistically at my own century, and so you should do. Love? Certainly, for a young man of your gifts, Alejandro, a young man who has borne other burdens of your century....why, certainly I believe, as any righteous man, that the marriage would not be unworthy before God. But it is before men that we are speaking of now Alejandro. Mexia...."

When he said her name I almost fell into the window. I caught my balance and listened harder.

"Mexia," he repeated, "is a beautiful and not unintelligent woman, and so I can understand your desire, Alejandro, any man's desire for her, I should say, but now I will be that priest who refuses."

For there were many goods, he explained, many kinds of good, and he wanted the broad good for Alejandro, a position which perhaps no other Indian of his century would obtain. It would be solitary there, like the priesthood. But they had had such remarkable accounts of him.

Alejandro's eyes seemed unchanged throughout the long speech, and he continued to sit stiffly.

Finally, Father Tollinare stood up, stretched himself, and looked as if he would come to the window. I ducked down. He closed the shutters and spoke of the moon being especially bright. Then he must have left, for I heard the door close. Or was it Alejandro who had left? The following day, however, when we came for the lessons, there was no Mexia to be found.

The Dance

While Dr. Johann was there, Entralgo gathered some of his slaves together and had us dance for him. Two of the men who were musicians were told to play, while two men and two women danced. My mother was known as one of the best dancers, so she was one of the women that Entralgo chose. In those days, as I've said, women often wore dresses that exposed their breasts or they simply wore skirts; the breasts, especially the breasts of a preto or mulatto woman, were not considered shameful. My mother and the other women were dressed in this fashion. The two men wore cotton trousers and white cotton shirts that were tied by a string at the neck and open at the front.

Other people on the plantation were allowed to stop their work and stand around and watch. There was pineapple and cassava to eat, which we were told that Dr. Johann had provided for us, as a gift in return for our allowing him to paint us. This seemed an odd expression to me, for none of us had allowed him anything. Yet I partook of the pineapple and cassava along with the others.

When the dancers entered, I noticed Dr. Johann's eyes widen when he saw my mother among them. He had that look again, as if she'd done something disrespectful--to him or herself I still didn't know. Then the men and women were dancing, raising their arms into the air, lifting their bare feet. A lot of the children on the sidelines raised their arms, too, as they watched, and so did I. Most of the grownups, though, just stood and simply watched. The dancers were the only ones who were smiling. The men looked as if they were delighted with the dance and with the women. The women had a similar expression; they were delighted and happy with the dance and with the men. But those who stood on the sidelines looked solemn, except for some of the children, who clapped their little hands and laughed.

I continued watching Dr. Johann. His eyes kept getting darker and darker. In fact, his whole face seemed darker. He'd brought his canvas and brushes out into the yard, but instead of painting anything, he simply stood there looking. Then after some minutes, he walked toward the dancers. He stood nearest my mother, standing very still. The dancers kept dancing, but there was more tension and uneasiness in their movements, particularly in my mother's, although she tried to maintain her look of ease and abandon. Then Dr. Johann stepped closer. I thought he was about to reach out and grab my mother, but Entralgo was beside him now and grabbed his arms, saying nothing. Then he nodded to the overseer, who unfolded his own arms and clapped his hands for the dancers to stop and for the people to get back to their work.

I stood there wondering about what I'd seen. The overseer scowled at me and clapped his hands. I ran to my mother. I reached for her hand, but she didn't take hold of mine. I walked beside her back to the hut, my hands at my sides. She bent to enter the low door of the hut and I walked in behind her. Inside she turned to look down at me, then she touched my arm. I stared up at her, then down at the shadow of her arm on my arm. She started to stay something, but instead she hugged me.

At night as I lay on my hammock, I saw the shadow of a man. It bent to enter the small hut. It went to my mother's hammock and touched her arm. It said it hadn't seen such dances before. It called the dance dissolute, vulgar, unreligious. It didn't want her doing such dances. I knew it was Dr. Johann's shadow. He said he didn't want any woman of his to do such dances.

My mother was silent. I strained to look, but it was dark and I couldn't tell how her expression was. I could only see the tilt of her head. She raised up a bit, looking. I wondered if he too wished to see her expression.

"*Your* woman?" she asked. "*Yours*?"

"As long as I'm here, you're mine. When I leave you can go back to being your own."

She laughed, then she said, "No woman is her own in this country, Sir."

He bent toward her. His shadow seemed to cover hers.

"This is a country where neither the women nor their daughters are respected. How is it in your land?"

His shadow left hers and he went out. I closed my eyes and slept. In my dreams, I thought another man had entered. He stood near her in silence, and like Dr. Johann had touched her arm.

"You're still true to me, Acaiba?" he asked.

"True?" she repeated, as if that were an impossible question.

"You still believe in me, don't you?"

"Yes," she whispered.

In my dream, my grandmother was standing in front of me wearing many things on her body--fans, palm branches, the feathers of ducks and peacocks. She was dressed in blue and white and she walked around very slowly and dignified, her head held high.

"Gold means nothing to them," she said. "Dignity is their most prized possession."

Then she began to make the movements of the ocean--soft, gentle waves, then violent ones. She arched her back and made waves of her hips. She was wearing yellow flowers in her hair, and her cheeks and lips were red.

"Have you been to the house of images?" she asked.

She lifted me up from the hammock and carried me about as if I were a feather, then she replaced me.

A man came in carrying pickaxes, hammers, and other tools. He kissed her briefly and they walked out together, laughing.

Fiestas

When Dr. Johann asked Father Tollinare to take him to see the dances of two tribes of Indians who were in that territory, my mother and I were permitted to go along with them, as well as two men, who carried their belongings and Dr. Johann's canvases, paints, and other art materials.

Father Tollinare and Dr. Johann walked in front, then came my mother and I, followed by the two men. We walked on a narrow path through the forest, sometimes in single file. The forest was damp and close and dark, the trees covered with trumpet vines. We walked for several hours before stopping at the edge of a clearing.

We didn't reveal ourselves to the Indians, although we could have, for these were not warriors, and they knew Father Tollinare. As always, there were more women and children than men, and they were all without clothes, and the women had long golden breasts. I stared at the women's breasts and the heavy, bulging muscles in the backs, arms and legs of the men. The men wore cloths around their private parts, but the women and children wore nothing even there. I stood near Dr. Johann as he motioned for his canvases and charcoal and began to sketch.

Soon I began watching his drawings more than the real people. I watched him sketch the long breasts of one of the women. She was bent forward slightly, carrying a basket across her back, and holding a child's hand. Her hair was long, straight, and black, and her cheekbones very high.

Father Tollinare stood by silently, solemnly. Sometimes I would look at him. He'd watch the Indians first, then watch Dr. Johann, then watch the cinnamon trees. Sometimes he'd leave us, go back a ways, then return. Since Mexia had disappeared, he was mostly silent now.

Dr. Johann drew a woman holding a child, another squatting with a baby sucking at her breasts. I wondered if the milk from golden breasts tasted golden. It was mostly the women he drew, but there was one man. In the drawing, the man didn't wear a loincloth. Dr. Johann drew his navel and then his heavy private part. I thought that Father Tollinare would say something, even at this, but he didn't.

Then four men came out into the clearing, carrying shields and spears. Dr. Johann stepped away from his canvas, looking startled and surprised. Father Tollinare whispered that the dance was beginning. Dr. Johann watched as the men danced a pretended fight. He kept watching. I waited for him to sketch them, but he didn't.

When the dance ended, and the men sat down exhausted, it was then I thought Dr. Johann would sketch them. But still he did not. Instead, he began to sketch a canoe and a running stream that wasn't even there. After that, the face of one of the women began to appear. Suddenly, she was sitting in the canoe holding her child.

We did not go into their camp. I wondered, though, what they'd have done if he'd showed them drawings of themselves. Would they have been pleased or alarmed?

On the way back through the forest, Dr. Johann wondered aloud also what they'd have thought, seeing themselves.

"That you were trying to conjure their spirits," Father Tollinare said, solemnly. Then he added in the same solemn voice, "By now they believe it's their destiny to have their spirits conjured."

Dr. Johann said nothing. He scratched his head. I pulled a wild fig from one of the trees and ate it.

At night when we were in our hut, when my mother had finished her laundry and her trip to see Dr. Johann, she sat in her hammock and began to tell me of something she remembered vaguely. She said that going to the place of the Indians had made her think of it. There was a long march and she was riding on the shoulders of a man. She was no more than two or three. But that part of the memory was very clear, and the people in the march were not her own people, but the people we'd just seen. They'd allowed my mother and my grandmother to journey with them.

"I don't know what it was all about," she said, swinging slightly in her hammock. "I kept feeling that they were protecting us, that it was for our protection that we went along with them. Perhaps we'd just escaped from some place and had gone to them for refuge. It must've been that."

As she talked, I pictured myself riding on the shoulders of one of the men I'd seen. Riding on his shoulder and eating a wild fig. But we weren't in a long march, not in a column. The line had formed not a column but a circle and so we were walking around in a circle. The people wore masks with sad faces, masks of people, of ducks, of horses, of strange animals I'd not seen before. I didn't know whether they were imaginary, magical animals or real ones. One man had his whole body covered with a cloth made of the bark of a cinnamon tree and he was painted with squares and triangles, but his real face was exposed. The man whose shoulders I was riding on was naked, fully, but I couldn't see his face. They began to walk faster and faster in the circle. The man asked me to hold tighter, because they were trying to protect us, me and "the crazy woman."

I held on as tight as I could, till I grew dizzy and let go and tumbled backward to the ground. Then he was bending over me, chanting something that was the repetition of one sound. I felt as if I were the center of a magical ritual but that nothing was demanded of me, except what destiny intended. He sang the same monotonous song again and again and his voice grew higher and higher, till it was octaves higher than any sound I'd ever heard, till it grew too high to hear. The same sound over and over. What the word meant I don't know.

Although he was bending over me, and this is the strange thing, it was still the back of his head that I saw, his straight hair, a feather, a fish-shaped gold ornament, strips of fur. I wondered how he could bend over me, and yet I could not see his full face. His voice grew higher and higher as before, then lower and more solemn. Then lower still. I waited for it to get too low to hear. But then he gave a great shout and lifted his arms in the air. Yet, it was still the back of his head that I saw, and sometimes the side of his face and one high cheekbone, but never did he turn toward me enough for me to see his full features.

Others lifted me onto his shoulders again. Although I'd fallen I had felt no pain. Again we were marching in the circle.

"Somehow I felt it was for our protection that we were with them," my mother was saying. "But I can't remember anything. I can't remember how we left them and got to this place. I can't remember anything about our movements in time or place. We were just here."

She climbed down out of her hammock and went to a corner of the hut. She came back and handed me a bowl of coconut milk. As I drank it I saw myself on the man's shoulders again, marching in the circle. A woman entered the circle, one of the women with long golden breasts, and they moved around her three times. Then someone lifted me from the man's back and placed me into the arms of the man. It was a man I knew. It was Alejandro, the man Father Tollinare had sent to study in Europe, the man who had absconded--it was Father Tollinare's word; I'd overheard him say it to Entralgo--with Mexia.

"You'll have to bear with me, my love," he was saying to me. "I'm a silent man, given to few sentences."

"What are you about, Almeydita? Your daydreams again?"

My mother stood over me. She picked up the bowl that was on the ground beside me. There was coconut milk all over me and my hammock and the ground.

"There's no more," she said.

Now it was I the woman in the circle, no little girl. Then the silent Alejandro took my hand and brought me into the hut.

When Dr. Johann went again to the Indian village, I didn't get to go along with them, but my mother went along with them, and when she returned repeated everything to me. At the village Dr. Johann had done more sketches. My mother described one of them to me: a sketch of a man with feathers decorating his body. He was raising a wooden sword and cracking the skull of another man. The strange thing was that nothing like that had occured while they were at the village. Not even a war dance.

"Tell me something about them?" Dr. Johann had asked Entralgo as they headed back.

"They used to eat each other, but they don't anymore. Even those they loved, they'd eat. When the Company of Jesus came, they converted them and changed their ways." Entralgo laughed and peeked at Father Tollinare and went on talking. "They're called Tupis, I mean Tapuyas. All theto do was eat and drink and kill. Now all they do is eat and drink. They don't fight anymore. They only eat Christian things. Now they're very courteous to each other, very loving. If only the Company of Jesus could do that for the rest of us, eh Father? But I bet, I'd swear to it--mustn't I swear?--that there's some amongst them who still remember the taste of human flesh. What do you think, Father?"

Father Tollinare, of course, said nothing. And my mother said that, although he was talking to Father Tollinare, he'd looked at her when he said that last thing, about the taste of human flesh. But she said that she herself had heard differently about the Tapuyas, that they were the enemies of the flesh-eaters and not human flesh-eaters themselves, and that they were always fighting those who ate human flesh.

"In that dance you saw," explained Entralgo, "they were only pretending, but in the old days it was real. Look at the wench, looking at me with eyes like a sea cow. I only tell what's true. I don't give false information. Do you still remember the taste of it? I bet if you don't the old woman does."

My mother had said nothing to this, though she had glanced at Dr. Johann who'd turned his back to her, so that she didn't see his face.

When no one was looking, she grabbed at one of the wild figs and chewed it fiercely.

What is Happening in Agriculture?

Entralgo sent my mother and me into the field to carry water to the slaves there. Some of them would stop, drink water, then return to the field. Antonia came up to us, and I handed her a gourd to drink from. Her eye was red and swollen. The master, I was sure, had beat her again.

I noticed that a young white man was out in the field, working along with the slaves. However, unlike the others, he'd stop at times to examine the weeds and other plants. I remember I'd seen him before, when I'd gone to the stream on the other side of the cane field to take laundry. I carried a small load on my head. He was stripped to the waist and washing himself, even his armpits. I ducked behind a bush and waited tilll he'd left the stream, before I came forward to wash my clothes.

Now I asked, "Who is that white man?"

"Maybe he's not a branco," said my mother.

"That's Entralgo's son, don't you know," said Antonia. "Your master's son, don't you know."

My mother laughed a cruel laugh.

"Not his son *that* way," said Antonia. She straightened her shoulders, took a long drink from the gourd, then said, "That there's his *legitimate* son, his 'boy,' who went off to study in Paris."

My mother said nothing. She took the empty gourd from Antonia and scooped more water out from the barrel, then handed it to her.

"Then why does he have him work in the field like a common slave?" she demanded. "If that's his boy-boy?"

While they talked, I kept staring at the pale boy whose brown, loose hair kept falling into his face. He wore a long-sleeved white shirt that opened at the collar, black trousers and sandals. Tuffs of brown hair peeked out at his collar.

"It's his choice," said Antonia.

"His choice? What d'you mean by that?"

"He's come to teach his father what's happening in Agriculture, new European ideas that'll help his father's crops grow larger and faster. As if they didn't grow large and fast enough."

I watched the boy. I remembered walking down the long path to the stream and being frightened that he'd reappear again. Hairs in his armpits.

"He'll fail," said Antonia, decisively.

"Who says that?" my mother asked. "Why do you say it?"

"He'll fail," repeated Antonia. She touched her swollen eye. She poured a bit of water in her palm and bathed the eye in it. "Here he is bringing new European ideas, but is it Europe here? It's not Europe here. It's new world ideas that've got to be brought in here. New world ideas," said Antonia.

She winked her swollen eye at me. My mother shook her head, saying nothing. Then she scooped the gourd into the barrel for another thirsty slave.

But it turned out to be true what Antonia, the so-called drunkard and thief, had said. Not only were the crops not larger and bigger, but they were smaller and more shriveled up and some did not come at all. After the disappointment, some said the son left and went back to Europe. Others said Entralgo drove him off, that the son had wanted to stay in the New World and keep trying, that he'd learn the right things to apply to Brazilian soils, but the father said no, he wouldn't allow him to experiment with his fields. Go help the farmers in Paris, he said. There're enough poor bugs in Brazil.

Still others said that the latter thing couldn't have happened, because they saw Entralgo standing in the yard shaking his son's swollen and bitten hands, hands that were a dry white color and still covered with blood and dust. And so the father had to take them very tenderly.

Those who claimed the latter said that if Entralgo sent his son away, it was done out of love and for his own good.

It was Antonia, however, who said he'd called his son a poor bug, as well. And it's probably true what she said, for after the poor bug left for Europe, she had another swollen eye.

Miss Pepperell and the Lice Scratcher

Entralgo's daughter lay her head in my lap. Her dark hair flowed to the floor, while I parted it and searched for lice. A strange white woman came into the room. She was whiter than any woman I'd seen so far in that country. She looked as if she was lost, but she kept staring at me. Entralgo's daughter turned her head to look at her, but said nothing. I combed my fingers through her hair again, but wouldn't look again at the white woman, who was almost as white as rice. I wondered how Entralgo's daughter felt with her head in my lap. The white woman left, then she returned and peeked at us again, then she left.

"Mistress, tell me, who is that woman?" I asked

"She's from England, from London. An introduction from the queen, no less. Well, one of the queen's retainers, but that's just as good."

I didn't tell her that I'd never seen a woman so white before.

"Her name's Miss Pepperell, of all things. She's very wealthy and she travels. She's very wealthy, that's all my father needs to know. He said she's from a very old and decadent family in London. I heard him say so. And to her face. But she only laughed and said something about 'an excess of traditions.' 'Not decadent,' she said, 'but an excess of traditions.' I don't know myself what they were talking about. It was some sort of joke, of course. My father fancies jokesters. But my father says she's been to Russia and to Africa and places of that sort and now she's come here. She's a writer of some sort. He's never been at all fond of lady writers. He thinks they all write nonsense. But she writes travel stories, and like I said, she's a jokester, and he likes that." She twisted her head in my lap. "But I don't want to talk about her. Tell me a story about an enchanted black woman. That's what I want to hear."

"I don't know any stories about enchanted black women."

"There used to be stories about enchanted black women. My mother said she was always told stories about enchanted Mooresses. All the time."

"The only women I know are ordinary," I said.

She looked disgusted, shook her head rapidly back and forth, put her hand under my knee and pushed hard.

"Maybe she'll put you in her book, you're so uppity," she said. "She was looking at you, anyhow. Hush."

The strange woman, Miss Pepperell, came back into the room, looked at us, at me especially, and left again.

The girl burst out laughing. "Soon they'll come for you, anyhow," she said.

"To the negro asylum?" I asked eagerly.

She said nothing. She picked a lice from her own hair and flicked it on the ground.

"Who for me?" I asked, then not to sound so uppity, I added, "Mistress, who for me?"

"A man's come here for the cure."

"The cure?"

She laughed again, jumped up from my lap and ran out. She was wearing nothing but her blouse and bloomers. I waited for her to return, but after a while, my mother came into the room carrying a butcher knife. She grabbed my hair and put the knife to my neck.

It was then that Entralgo and a stranger entered. The stranger looked frightened, but Entralgo's face was hard and expressionless. Then he chuckled. My mother said in an even voice that unless they stopped their plans with me, she'd kill me.

Entralgo looked expressionless again. The stranger, in embarrassment asked, "You're sure she's a virgin, are you, Sir?"

"Yes," said Entralgo. "Yes."

Entralgo started to come near.

"No," said my mother. "You'll not take my daughter."

That was the first time I'd seen my mother behave that way. She was big-boned, but at the same time a very delicate and gentle woman.

"They say that only a virgin can cure this man," Entralgo stated. "I want Almeydlta."

He still looked at my mother. The stranger reached down and scratched his genitals as though there were lice there.

"I'll kill mine as surely as you'd kill yours if this were to happen. Would you give your daughter up to such a man?"

The stranger came to Entralgo and whispered something.

Entralgo said to him angrily, "Who's the slave here?"

The stranger whispered again.

"Who's the slave here?" asked Entralgo.

I could see behind them the girl standing outside the door with her hair flowing, and a look of amusement on her face. When her father turned, she ran.

My mother took the knife from my neck and held my head against her stomach.

"Who's the slave here?" asked Entralgo again. "Why, we'll see who's the slave here."

When we returned to the hut, my mother explained to me what had happened. At first she intended not to explain, but I kept asking her. Then she told me that it was believed that the blood of a black virgin would cure men with certain diseases. I thought of all the ways he could get my blood. Then she explained to me about the way in which a virgin's blood is drawn by a man.

I sat on my hammock looking at her, very still, with my eyes wide. She stopped talking suddenly, then she looked as if there was something she would tell. I kept waiting, but she refused to tell me that thing.

"This is why you've not been bothered before now," she said, looking at me. "There are gentlemen in this territory who know they can always count on Master Entralgo for such cure."

That was when she mixed a certain herb and gave it to me to drink. I didn't know what it was for, I simply watched her boil the water, then remove the clay jug. She put a dried root in it and covered it with a banana leaf, then she waited. When the water was very dark, she gave it to me to drink. She watched me until I had drunk it all down.

"Here begins Miss Pepperell's travels and travails in Recife and other territories in the wild country of Brazil, 1680," read the first page of the notebook.

One of the women who cleaned Miss Pepperell's room after she'd left Entralgo's found a notebook and rather than give it to Master Entralgo to send to Miss Pepperell wherever she might be, had given the book to my mother, knowing that she was literate and also had a daughter who was at Father Tollinare's school. My mother gave the notebook to me, because she did not read English. She'd barely learned Portugese and Latin. But she knew that I not only read Portuguese and Latin, but that Father Tollinare, experimenting with the new generation of students was teaching us our choice of several of the "vulgar tongues." Because I'd once overheard Father Tollinare's telling someone how books in English, more than any other language, were often banned by the Holy Office of the Inquisition, chose to learn that language. In those days, it was strange for a slave to be able to choose anything. So I chose that language readily. However, it was only years later that I was able to translate the notebook fully.

The entries were not stories, not those "vices" as the holy fathers called them, but rather thoughts that Miss Pepperell had while staying at Entralgo's and perhaps notes for future articles and letters she'd write and send to the London newspapers.

Under the first title she'd scribbled, but drawn a line through "Tales of an Englishwoman Abroad," then she'd written and also drawn a line through "In the Americas, 1680." I'll include here a sampling of what the notebook contained, though as I say, it was only years later that I was able to translate it fully as I present it here:

Sometimes it all seems like a fine parade and comedy, even the so-called society here in Brazil. Exaggerated characteristics. But there are people here of great character, as our English men and women. Sometimes I think, though, that if they were placed on a London street, they'd be seen as mere clowns and jesters. But I wonder, how am I seen? Mr. Entralgo entertains me with chocolates and conversation.

Sometimes I can't tell the mulatto serving women from the daughters of the house. They are all tawny people. I suppose it is because of the intensity of the sun. But it is the same as in New Spain. Often to be "white" here is merely to consider oneself white, or to be considered so by others. I have embarrassed myself at least several times treating a mulatto woman as if she were a mistress of the house. I must add that the women, all of them, go around in pantaloons and bare feet when they are inside the house. How can one distinguish one class from the other when they are all in pantaloons?

There's been a gentleman visitor here rotten with venereal disease who wants one of the little slave girls. Disgusting. He has got none so far, and if off to another plantation. I must jot down the name of it. Corricao's. A gentleman? Did I call him a gentleman? But I've heard them whisper that even the priests are rotten with it here.

I ride on horseback. This is a country of enchantment. The Indians, at least the ones near here, are not so fearsome as those in some of the countries I have been to. They are quite handsome people. Golden.

Entralgo sees me talking to a slave man and calls me in. I swear he was a mulatto and I thought he was surely one of the gentlemen residing here, with a letter of introduction. I did intentionally talk to another slave man, though, while Entralgo wasn't looking. I was listening to some of his remedies. There are all sorts of herbs and spices here that seem to have *quite useful purposes. I wish I were a better naturalist. Entralgo says that in my country and some other countries that I've been, I may be a gentlewoman, but here such behavior can only be considered the behavior of a whore.*

I have lice scratched from my head. I observed it being done. It feels quite pleasurable. So relaxing. Lice is everywhere.

As a woman, I'm shown little respect here. I used to think that people who hid their women respected them, but it's not so, at least not here. Or perhaps it's because I'm too much in evidence that they show me little respect. Oh, yes, I should have guessed it. Because I'm not here on the arms of a husband.

I've spoken too freely with one of the servants again and shown her every politeness. It's because of my fascination with that medicine man and she promised to take me to witness one of his purification rituals. But alas, he won't allow me to witness it. Even so, I had to explain to Entralgo that my interest is mainly in something that will go into the newspapers, that I have no personal interest in all of it. Even when I show him my sketch of the man to go along with the article "My Conversations with a Medicine Man," he still disapproves. He looks at me as if I'm some new scandal in the world and says I'm not the woman of good family described in my letter of introduction and whose father he remembers dining with in Lisbon.

I tell him that this is the only way that I can finish my collection of sketches on the Indians and Negroes. But he fears I'm a bad influence on his wife and daughters and takes me in hand. He speaks again of my old and decent family, but I know he really thinks it's an old and decadent one. He's as much as told me so. And to my face.

I receive a slap in the face and an accusation. All very scandalous. He concludes I'm a whore, though in the beginning he liked my wit. A whore? His wife calls me a poor unfortunate woman. A very unsettling scene, and in the presence of Dr. Johann, a likable man. He (Entralgo) says he doesn't want a woman here who might be the ruin of his daughter whom he has given every care and attention. So I must abandon my articles on the Indians and the Negro Medicine Man and the Women here. I cannot utter one word in my defense. Any white woman who's been to Africa, he says. But my fortitude remains.

I'll return to New Spain and seek sanctuary with the Barbacotes. Is that their name? Or perhaps I should go visit the Corricao plantation first. Titles for articles: A Brief Conversation with a Medicine Man, A Woman of Society in Recife, I Miss the Church of England, Chocolate and Coffee, Notes on Good Behavior in this Country, Some Questions I've Been Asked About England Here and Answers I Have Given, Are There Any Free Negroes Anywhere? My Conversations with an Indian Medicine Woman, What It Means To Be An Ungentlewoman Here, Some Anecdotes, Among Strangers, Strange Men and Women in the Americas.

Sacred River

When we left the circle and went into the hut, he lay me in his hammock. I waited, not knowing what would happen. He began drawing lines on his face--moons and half moons, many connected squares and lines down his neck. Just above his shoulders he began drawing arrows or what resembled arrows. Then he looked at me solemnly. When he got near me, he held my hands and together we watched the blood flow from my fingers.

My mother lowered her basket to the ground, then she picked up my clothes that had fallen, and placed them back in my tiny basket, and placed it securely on my head again.

"I don't know what to make of you, Almeydita," she said. "When will this spirit stop entering your head? They'll think that you're crazy too. Do you want them to send you to a negro asylum too?"

I held my hands around the rim of the basket, as we went down to the river.

"For the Indians this is a sacred river," she said softly. "But for Entralgo, it's just any river."

I said nothing. I thought she would tell me what the river meant, but she didn't. *When I got to the edge of the water I placed the tips of my fingers in it. He helped me wash the blood from my fingers and the wounds closed instantly. He said now the marriage ceremony had been completed and he kissed me.*

When I finished my laundry I asked my mother if I might go visit Tempo, and she said yes. I raced up the side of the mountain. He did not smile at me as before. He looked at me solemnly as he held onto the bridle of one of the horses. When I saw him look so solemn, I did not run to get onto the horse, but stood very still.

"How are you today, Almeydita?" he asked.

I nodded, then I said I was fine.

"Are you the same today as you were yesterday?"

I said yes. I must have looked at him strangely.

"Don't you want your ride today?" he asked with a smile.

I waited for him to ask the old question, but he didn't.

Again, I stood very still, looking up at him.

"Aren't you going to ask about my mother?" I demanded. "Don't you want me to tell her anything?"

He said he'd tell her himself. I must've been looking at him strangely again, for he gave me my strange look back. Then I stared down at his riding boots. Finally, I walked down the hill to where my mother was, lifting her basket of laundry onto her head and nodding toward mine.

Mercado

"Where are we going?" I asked, as we got into the same wagon that my grandmother had ridden away in. "Are we going to the negro asylum too?"

She said that we were not. She looked expressionless, then solemn. Although there was straw on the floor of the wagon, where we placed our backs was hard. Three silent men also sat in the wagon. They were not from our plantation, but we were all on our way to the same place, wherever it was to be.

"Where are we going?" I pestered her again.

She didn't answer.

"You're going to market," said one of the men.

My mother looked at him but didn't change her expression.

"What would you like?" he asked. "National or international travel? Would you like to go to North America, little girl? How about Cuba?"

"Russia," I said. "Or England."

My mother looked at me. The man laughed.

"What about back to Africa?" he asked. "What about back to the Old Country?"

"They don't sell you back there," I said.

He laughed again. I looked at him closely and then I remembered. I'd seen him once before when my mother had been allowed to go into town with Entralgo's wife who was going to visit her cousin but taking her own servants with her. We'd seen him crossing the street. He was wearing a dark coat and a white ruffled shirt and dark trousers like a white student or licenciado would wear, and he even wore buckled shoes. Though he was wearing only cotton trousers with a rope belt now, I knew it was the same man. Entralgo's wife had laughed when she saw him and so did the black driver. Later, when I asked my mother why they'd laughed at the man, she explained that they always laugh whenever a black man dresses 'out of his color.' It had been the first time I'd seen such a black man, and I'd turned my head all the way around to look at him, but I hadn't laughed.

"Why?" I'd asked.

"I don't know," she confessed.

"You didn't laugh," I said.

"No," she replied.

Entralgo's wife had asked the driver who the silly man was. The driver answered that he was a black school teacher in the town. The mistress had laughed again, for on the plantations there was no such thing. She'd never heard of such a thing. The driver explained that he was a tutor to many white students in the town. The mistress laughed again, a deeper laugh, and exclaimed that such an absurdity could happen only in the city, which she considered an immoral place anyhow.

I glanced at my mother, who did not seem to recognize the man. Every now and then, though, as we journeyed, I'd sneak another look at him. He was wearing dark trousers and a plain white shirt, but was as barefooted as any slave.

The wagon stopped in front of a long barn and we were told to go inside. Before we'd left the plantation, they'd taken our garments and given us two wide pieces of cloth. My mother didn't cover her breasts with it, only the lower part of her body. Her breasts were large and firm. I too put my cloth around my waist and knotted it, but it hung below my knees.

The three men sat on the floor of the barn with others who were already there. My mother remained standing and so did I. A strange white man came to the doorway and peeked in at us. I crossed my arms about my chest, as if I were a branca, even though I had no breasts then. I looked at my mother. But, like I said, in those days it was not shameful for a preto woman to show her breasts. I myself had only learned shame while in the casa grande. My mother did not cover her breasts as I had done, although she was the one that the stranger watched, and the only one.

He had dark slick hair like Dr. Johann, and I began to wonder whether Dr. Johann knew that my mother and I had been taken away to market and whether he himself would come to purchase us. So I imagined it was Dr. Johann standing there considering what price he'd give for us, instead of the stranger. In my mind, I questioned him.

"I heard you say that when you left my mother would no longer be your woman. But she's the one who's leaving, who's being sold away, even before you've had your chance to. How do you feel about her now, Sir? How do you look at her now? Is she still your woman?"

He wouldn't answer, although he kept watching my mother as if she were the only one there, or as if there was some power she possessed that drew his eyes to her.

There were straw mats on the floor that the three black men had sat down upon. One was filing his toenails with the edge of a small stone, the other was chewing on a piece of reed he'd picked up from the floor. The third man who looked like the black school teacher I'd seen crossing the street in town sat with his knees drawn up, his arms across his knees, his face in his arm, staring at the ground. None of them seemed to know that my mother and I were there. They didn't look at us at all.

It seemed strange that they'd let my mother keep a certain wide hat and long earrings that she was wearing, and that she said a certain man had given to her. I don't know what certain man she meant. If it were Dr. Johann I'm sure she'd have said so. But she kept them almost as if they were charmed. I watched her and then I looked at the white man again, who was still watching her. He kept staring at her face, her breasts, her smooth round shoulders. She still didn't look at him, and her eyes seemed vacant. I don't know how long it was that he stood in the doorway, his arms folded. He was wearing a loose white shirt and trousers, but of a fine well-cut material. I didn't think it was strange then the kind of hat my mother was wearing, but it was not a slave's hat.

Finally, the man who stood in the doorway left, and then in the evening another man came to get my mother, for she'd been sold. Before she left with him, she put her face against mine. I could feel her soft breasts against my shoulder. I could smell the oil in her hair.

Behind her the stranger reappeared in the door, and the man who'd come for her pulled her away from me. Her eyes remained vacant as though she'd pushed them beyond tears. I stood very still as the water dropped from my eyes. The black man who'd been the teacher and who had his head in his arms looked up at me, then he patted the ground beside him. I went and sat down, but he said nothing to me. He put his hand on my chin and touched the side of my face and wiped the tears away, but still he said nothing.

I sat with him a long time in silence and then I heard something that sounded like, "They drink the hair of Indians," but it made no sense and must've been those words you form when you're sleeping. Every now and then the man would reach out and touch my shoulder, but he wouldn't speak to me.

"Where are the new negroes?" I heard someone call.

Others came and stood in the doorway.

"The woman was sold, but the little girl, she's still…"

"The brutality of existence," the man whispered, touching my shoulder and leaning toward me.

"The brutality of existence," he repeated. "That's what I'll call myself when they ask my name again. Brutalidade da Existencia. I'm no longer Matoso. If they ask you, "Who's this man?' you must tell them, 'Brutalidade da Existencia.'"

I was the one who was pulled up from the ground. I looked at him as I was going, but his head was on his knees again and he wouldn't look at me.

"Brutalidade da Existencia," I said, but he wouldn't look up.

I was put into the same wagon I'd been brought here in. As we traveled, I recognized the landscape. It wasn't to a new place I was being taken, but to an old one. I was put into the hut of my mother. I waited to be told what had occurred to me, but no one came, and so I climbed into my hammock and fell asleep.

Virgin of the Stones

I was lying in the hammock when he came back into the hut. He'd washed the lines from his face and neck and had oiled his whole body until it was slick and shining. This time he didn't make my fingers bleed, but climbed into the hammock with me.

"Is this the same girl?"

"Yes, she'd the same one."

"And a virgin?"

Something hard and soft and firm scraped against my belly. Then I felt my mother's breasts against my shoulder again.

"What's wrong with the girl?"

"What do you mean?"

He began to curse. I felt him moving between my knees.

"I can't enter her. She won't be entered. It keeps pushing me out. It's like trying to penetrate a stone."

A finger on my stomach, touching me between my legs. The man cursed again, said the names of holy saints, called on the Virgin of Solitude, then said Entralgo's name.

"What's wrong with her?" he repeated.

He got out of the hammock; it swung heavily. The two shadows of men left the hut. I touched myself between my legs, but felt no stone there.

"I'll have her examined. I'll have the old woman examine her."

The man cursed again, saying that he'd waited for that one because he'd wanted that one. He'd wanted it to be a pleasure as well as a cure. But he'd waited long enough.

"I'll have the old woman look at her."

"Why's it that only a black one can cure such a malady?" he asked. He cursed again, and then he called the name Corricao. I'd heard that name before, but felt certain it wasn't the name of a saint.

Entralgo was silent, then he said something that I couldn't make out.

"In the condition I am in at the moment…"

"…then it is best that you leave."

In the morning, an old woman whose name I didn't know and who refused to have anyone call her anything, except "old woman" if it was necessary (and the story was that even when she was young she refused to be called anything at all, except "woman," when that was necessary). I was silent when she entered and I was silent too when she spread my legs open and began to touch me.

"Am I going to die?" I asked.

"No, you're not going to die," she said sternly, although she looked at me as if she knew something that I didn't. Then she left the hut and returned with a bowl and cloth. First she wiped my stomach and then she wiped the parts between my legs carefully again and again.

Entralgo entered while my legs were spread. I tried to close them, but the old woman without a name held them open. Entralgo looked between them as though he were seeing nothing, or something that he'd seen many times. Then he leaned forward as if seeking something.

"What's wrong with her?" he asked.

The old woman was silent.

He waited, but didn't press her.

"It's a rare thing," she said when she was ready to speak. "I've only seen it once, though I've heard tales of it. Perhaps some have a name for it, but I don't. There's something that has made the muscles here so they won't give." She touched. "So they won't give at all. See how they contract tighter when I...If there's a name for it, I don't know it."

Entralgo was sllent. I tried to shut my legs, thinking that he might try to touch me there too, but the old woman held them open. She cooed at me.

"Does it sound strange to you?" she asked Entralgo.

He kept staring at the place he'd seen many times, and then at the place where he sought something. Finally, he asked, "When she's a woman, will she grow out of it?"

"I've only seen it once, and heard tales of it. But they say it's a condition that stays with a woman."

Entralgo said nothing. He got closer to me and touched me himself. I squirmed, but the old woman held me. When he was satisfied there might be some strange truth in what she was saying, he left. Though before he left, he gave me a look I couldn't read. But it was still the look of someone seeking something.

"He's gone to wash his hands and then he'll go to the chapel," said the old woman. She wiped me again and then pushed my legs together. "I've seen this only once," she said, looking at me closely. "I've heard tales of it and I've told tales of it. When I tell my tales, I tell them that it's what the gods do to protect certain women whom the devil desires. But I didn't do this. I'm not responsible for this. Who did this? Who gave you the secret plant? Who knows the secret plant but me?"

Vision and the Woman Without a Name

Shortly after my mother had been sold, Tempo disappeared from the mountainside along with his saddle horses. Now I took my mother's huge laundry basket down to the stream, except now there was no play, no bounding up the hillside to speak with Tempo, or ride one of his horses.

I carried my laundry down to the stream and squatted beside the old woman without a name. She must've read my thoughts, because she said, "Tempo no longer keeps his saddle horses on the mountain."

I nodded.

"Who'll make you race to the sky now?" she asked.

"No one," I said.

The woman laughed.

I saw a man and woman on the side of the mountain, and the man embraced her. But by now I was used to such daydreams and paid them no mind.

"Did you think they were strangers?" she asked, looking at me askance, as she scrubbed her own laundry. "Can't you tell when a man and woman have come a long journey together?"

I looked at her. She was a thin dark woman with straight gray hair. Perhaps she was part Tupi, I don't know. I looked back at the side of the mountain. The man and woman were not there. I moved the clothes back and forth in the stream.

"A man has many spirits and so does a woman."

I said nothing, but now I felt that I was beside my grandmother again, and wondered why they'd not taken this other crazy woman away.

"A madwoman and the daughter of the daughter of a madwoman," she said, reading my thoughts again.

"Has he followed her? Has Tempo followed my mother to the other plantation?" I asked hurriedly. "Is that why he's not here? Did he love her dearly and follow her?"

The woman without a name laughed. "If a man disappears, he must reappear somewhere."

I rinsed a girl's underclothes. One of Entralgo's daughter's. In my mind I saw Tempo on the side of another mountain and my mother racing to meet him. Then he got on one of his horses, lifted her to the back of it and they rode off.

The old woman looked at me, not askance, but fully. "Come on and shoulder your burden," she said. "It's time to get back."

She lifted her basket of clothes onto her head. I raised my own. I held my hands on the sides of the basket. She walked with hers sitting freely. Her hair was so straight I wondered how she could balance it. I stared at the muscles in her legs. They were the muscles of a younger woman. As we walked, I kept straightening my basket.

"When you become a woman," she began.

"What?" I asked.

She didn't answer. We followed the other women and watched the steam rise from trees. When the clothes were dry, we folded them into baskets.

There was one thing that the woman without a name would never mention, and that was when she had come to examine me. She behaved as if it were not a thing that had happened in the world.

Even when I asked her what was Entralgo seeking, she pretended not to know.

Dreams

"Why is it that you have no name?" I asked her.

"Oh, I'm sure that I've got one, but it's unknown to me. But what've you come for?"

She was sitting on the floor of her hut smoking a long pipe. I sat across from her.

"What have you dreamt?" she asked, before I told her why I'd come.

"Three white men in a boat and the other boat had seven black men. The black men had round heads and wore white loincloths. The white men were wearing white hats and white suits. The two boats were close to each other and the men were looking at each other. Then there were two white men sitting at a table and two white men standing. They were dressed in dark suits. Three black men naked, except for cloths around their loins, were standing in front of them, waiting. The black men had marks on their faces, stars and dots. Their faces were solemn. They didn't speak the language of the men they stood in front of. I saw the side of one of the men's faces. His cheeks, his temples, his forehead were painted. When he turned toward me, I saw the marks from his head to the tip of his nose. He looked at me without seeing me, and then he turned back to the men at the table. I felt he'd been a man of power somewhere."

She was silent, then she said, "Describe them."

"What?"

"The scars on the man's face."

"Long slashes, a six-pointed star with dots between the points, a half circle with long slashes inside."

I made the marks on the ground.

She watched but said nothing.

"I'm an old woman who's lost her name and has no memory of such markings," she said. "I'm no interpreter of dreams."

"They told me..."

"How old are you, Almeydita?"

"Fifteen."

"An age where you bind your breasts...But me, I'm no interpreter of dreams. I could sound out your future in your voice, in your eyes, when you are older, read it in the lines of our forehead. But I'm no interpreter of dreams. What do you see now?" she asked, looking at me and holding my chin.

"Nothing?"

"A man touching the side of my face, my hair, my shoulders."

"I knew it," she said. "What is he telling you?"

"He says that I still have the dreams of a slave. That now I'm in that place and I'm free."

"I knew it. But tell me which place, what place are you in?"

"He says only 'that place.' I look away from him. I feel as if I've strings on my thighs. No, they're scratches."

"Like in the Old Country?"

"No, scratches from branches, from walking through the forests, a great distance. He tells me that my mother and my grandmother..."

"What?"

"I don't understand what he's saying."

"What do you hear?"

"I don't understand what he's saying."

"What do you think you understand?"

I say nothing.

"What else does he say?"

"The same thing. He repeats it. That I am in that place and a free woman...I look at him, study the side of his face, the marks that have been put there. I don't know their meaning. These are not scratches. But scarification. Like you said. Like in the Old Country. I want to know their meaning. I ask him, but he won't tell me."

"Do you see the white woman, the branca?"

"White woman? Which white woman?"

She waits.

"Yes, I see her. A black man, a big one, brings her into camp."

"What camp? Are you sure it's a camp?"

"I don't know. It looks like a camp. In this part. But over there, there are houses."

"Who's she? Who is the woman? Tell me more about her."

"She's a branca yes, but she's dressed like an African woman. She's wearing an African garment."

"What else?"

"That's all. The man again, touching my face. What else? I don't know. Ah, yes. A black man and woman in a boat facing each other."

"Tell me more about the white woman."

"Only that I see her walking and she has long hair and is wearing an African garment. And there's a tall black man beside her."

"The one who's touched you?"

"No, another one. A ruler. He seems to be a ruler. His hair is long, it sticks up tall on his head."

"What else?"

"Nothing else. Yes, there are many palm trees."

She keeps her hand on my chin.

"Have you entered the dance with the other women?"

"I'm running. I enter the dance with the other women. Young women. I have no breasts."

"You're a woman and you have no breasts? Already you are binding them."

She touches the cloth around my bosom and puts her hand on my forehead and jaw.

"I watch their breasts and their round protruding bellies, and the dark between their thighs. I can't explain what I don't have. A man follows me into the dance of the women. A young man. On the outside is a naked old man with a white beard. The women, everyone of them but me, must touch the beard of the naked old man. I want to run from the place where the women are dancing, but the man won't let me go. He says he wants to kiss my belly and squeeze my knees. The women shout and dance in a circle."

"Where've you learned this dance?"

"From the Dutch and the Portuguese, they say."

"What's the dance for?"

"The sacrifice of women. Women taken prisoner. I run."

"Are you a woman now?"

"Yes. The man tells me I must leave the new place...The women dance in a circle, holding a rope to their shoulders and waists. Now I'm a girl again. My mother braids my hair. She pushes her palm into my back.

I'm frightened. She pushes me into a long room full of men waiting to buy us. 'I want to remember my knees riding on his shoulders, my small hands wrapped around his chin,' she says. 'I want to remember the men with shoulders like birds.'"

"What? What are you saying now?"

"'The Indians found us and took us with them on their big march. The white men came, killed the Indian men, took the Indian women. I held my chin against my mother's head. They didn't kill us because we're useful and could be sold for much money. It was the Indians who were no longer of use.'"

"You've taken me from the future to the past, my child. Where are you now?"

"At a place where they wear the skin of anteaters and wood piercing their lower lips."

"You're still here, my child. You are back here now," she said, rubbing my arms.

I opened my eyes. She told me I would soon be leaving that place, Entralgo's plantation, and taken to a larger place.

"But still one doesn't enter or leave any place easily, or from will," she said, smoking her long pipe. "Not when one is a slave."

She grew very silent, then she reached out and took my arm, in anger. I had never seen such silence before, silence with anger at the core of it.

"So I'm the one you come to when you've dreams to tell," she said. "But soon you'll go to another woman. Soon you'll take them elsewhere. Soon you'll take your dreams to a woman who has a name. A name, yes, but a name which is not her own."

She laughed, then she held her arm up. I stood up and left her hut.

When I was outside, she called me from the doorway, "Almeyda!"

I turned.

But she only wished to say my name, my new name. I was not the little one now, not Almeydita. But Almeyda, the woman.

Mercado

I was taken to a large place with three arches over the doorway. The center arch that ran over the door was narrow and there were two wide arches over the windows, on either side of the narrow door. I didn't notice this until I was sitting. Then I looked up and saw a Madonna with a child over the doorway. And there were points of light over the doorway too.

I was afraid to look up at the people. There were many people. A white man stood in the center of the room with his hair in a braid. He wore a tall white hat and a long white coat. He was the only white man in the room. A mulatto sat at a narrow table counting money. He was not dressed as elegantly as the white man, but he had on trousers and a vest. A black woman dressed like a branca and wearing a long white dress and red shawl sat in a chair near the doorway with a basket of fruit in her lap. I heard people say that she was the woman of he white man who was standing.

The rest of us sat on mats on the bare floor. I sat beside a woman holding a baby. I watched her. I watched the baby. And there was a woman standing with her hands on her hips. I followed her eyes to a man painting pictures on the wall. In the picture I see the faces of the people around me. Dr. Johann, I wonder. I raise up to peer at him. But even from the back I know it's Dr. Johann. And he'd have his canvases. No crude painting on a wall. But I see the face of the woman standing. When she first entered, I saw anger in her face and then she sat down calmly, to wait with the others.

After a while, I lay on my stomach and watched the baby put his fingers in the woman's mouth. A man entered. The man in the white hat came over to where we were sitting and lifted a young boy, and brought him to the man who inquired his price. He spoke loudly.

"How much?"

He was told a price.

"As much as that, eh?"

He touched the boy's chin and the place in his pants where his genitals were.

"As much as that , eh?" he repeated.

Then he went to the table where the mulatto was counting money. He handed gold coins to the white man who then gave money to the mulatto. The man who'd purchased him took the boy and left. I rose from my stomach and sat on my knees. I turned and saw my face among the pictures on the wall and the man who'd painted it turning to watch me. No, not Dr. Johann at all. A wild, scoundrel's face, but shy eyes.

I don't know how long I sat there. No one spoke. The men and women sat watching each other and saying nothing. Resting on my elbows, I was lying between a certain silent man and woman. Every now and then the baby would look at me with his round quiet eyes. He looked as if he knew everything that was going on.

"I was one of the Ambassadors sent to him from Palmares," the man said to the woman.

I looked at him intensely, as I'd heard the name of that place.

"There were two other Negroes. I stood behind them. I clasped my hands before me, but I didn't fall on my knees as the men before me did. That's why I wasn't killed, but sold into slavery. Do you think that's why?

Me, I think so. Because I didn't fall on my knees, that's why. There was a black man dressed in boots and a long coat, a feather in his cap, serving as interpreter. I don't remember which man was governor then. Perhaps it was de Almeida. I don't know. My memory's gone."

The woman was silent. She touched the baby's head and continued to look at the man.

"There you'd be a free woman," he said. "There I'd have my memory again."

I looked at his black hair and the wrinkles under his eyes. I couldn't tell his age.

"I want to feel that place in my bosom," the woman said. She held the baby against her heart. The man looked at her, his eyes larger, solemn.

"I'm not the man to ask. Nhouguge is not the one. My memory's gone. I've only the muscles in my back and arms. My arms reach for cane. They don't reach for a woman anymore. Eh, that would be the place for you, and you'd wear your freedom in your eyes." He scratched his chin. "Perhaps it was de Almeida. I don't remember the one who was governor, but the one whose name I don't remember sent me to this place. Perhaps It was de Almeida."

I put my hands to my ears. The baby began to laugh. The woman looked down at him and kissed his head. The man who'd been painting me came and bent down. No, he was not Dr. Johann. Not with his rascal's face, and his eyes weren't so shy up close.

"Come and sit by me," he asked.

I got up and walked with him over to the mural.

"I want to get the lines of the eyes better," he said. "What were they talking about?"

But he was as inquisitive as Dr. Johann and he asked a thing instead of demanding it.

"A place called Palmares," I answered. "A place where black men and women are free."

He raised an eyebrow, but said nothing.

"Do you know the place?" I asked him, for I realized now that he was not a dark-skinned branco, but a mulatto.

"It's near the forest of Alagoas," he said. "Go into the Mundahu valley and come out again. Do you know the Barriga mountain range?"

"I don't know those places."

"Well, maybe they'll search you out," he said. He looked at me carefully. "They have spies everywhere. Perhaps one will take note of you."

I said nothing.

"I am Antalaquituxe," he said.

It was a Tupi name. Perhaps he was made up of everyone in this new world.

I told him my name was Almeyda.

He said nothing. Up close he did not seem like such a scoundrel. And his eyes were shy again. I sat down on the ground and looked up at him as he drew the mural. He was dressed like the other black men, loose white trousers and a shirt open at the front.

"They look like perfect hieroglyphs," he said.

"What?"

"Your eyes."

He put his hand to my chin and turned my face to the side.

"And from the profile you look like bastet."

I frowned, looking at his long nose and chin. It was only his huge eyes that were really handsome.

"What are you calling me?" I asked meanly.

"Bastet. The Egypian goddess. The goddess of love and joy. Or would you rather be Oshun, Shango's wife?"

My frown softened, but I still looked at the ugly man with suspicion. I'd heard of the Yorubaland warrior Shango from my grandmother, and though he'd been a brave and generous and loving man, his end had been tragic. I thought of the saints in Father Tollinare's stories, who dreamed and prayed for martyrdom. Their heroic dreams, their dreams of prophecy delighted me, but their dreams of martyrdom frightened me. I thought them silly.

Antalaquituxe painted my eyes larger than they were in reality and my eyes stared out into the room of people.

"Why've the white men made you do this? Paint all of us?" I asked.

"Why's it always the white men?" he asked with anger. "Why do you think it's the white man's idea?"

I was silent. I looked at him. He looked at me. No, not a scoundrel's face. HIs expression softened. He continued painting.

"Are you a spy of Palmares?" I asked.

"I'm waiting to be sold the same as you," he replied.

He drew the dark lines out until they touched my temples.

"I'm just passing the time doing this," he said. "Someone will buy you quickly, but this frog-faced man will be here a while."

I saw a shadow on the mural and turned. The man in the white hat was standing over me. Behind him was a white man waiting to examine me, and to offer a price.

"This is the one that I was told about?" he inquired.

"There've been others who've inquired of her, even Corricao, the breeder, but I've explained to them the situation…" He winked at the man.

The man waved his hands in the air, looking disgusted. "I grow cassava, and if she has good hands, that's all I need."

"Hold out your hands," said the man in the white hat.

I held out my hands.

"It's too bad, because this one is such a beauty."

The man who grew cassava said nothing as he examined my palms and the backs of my hands.

He didn't even ask my price, but when he was told it, he gave money at the table and I was taken out of that place.

"What is your name?" he asked when we were outside.

"Almeyda," I told him.

"Like the governor," he said matter-of-factly.

"Not with an 'i', with a 'y'," I said.

He looked at me. I'd forgotten that most slaves did not even know how to spell their own names and that it was best that they shouldn't. I looked down at my hands.

"I grow cassava," he repeated, and climbed onto his horse.

For a moment I thought that he would reach down and pull me up behind him, and I started to lift up my hand, but his horse pranced forward, and I trotted along after.

"I see you are one of Father Tollinare's experiments," he said quietly. "I see you will have to learn your proper place in the world."

Cassava

He took me to a black woman who dressed me in a long skirt and white blouse and tied a white rag around my head. She fixed the blouse so that it hung off my shoulders. Then she stood back and looked at me. She looked at my eyes and my shoulders.

"You're very pretty," she said.

Then she went to a corner of the small room and took from a box a string of beads with many different colors on them: yellow, red, black, blue, green, turquoise, white. She put them carefully around my neck. They hung down below my waist. She put them around my neck again, so that they doubled. She looked at me.

"There," she said, smiling.

She was tall with a thin waist and pretty eyes and her white blouse fell lower off her shoulders, showing the tips of her breasts. At that moment she was the woman I wanted to be when I became one.

I looked down at the floor that was not tile but ground packed hard together. I looked back up at her and smiled. She didn't give me shoes as she herself was not wearing any. She touched my shoulder and told me to come with her. I followed her to a barn with a wheel and a hot furnace. There were rollers connected to the wheel. Standing over a white stone pot were two young women dressed like the woman I'd followed, and there was an old woman in a long dress that did not show her breasts but came high on her shoulders. On the other side, a woman was baking bread over the fire, while a man knelt beside her, feeding coal into the furnace, and shielding his eyes. He was bare to the waist and had only a cloth around his loins. A man in striped pants and vest and a big white hat came to us when we entered. The woman stood looking at him without smiling. He pointed to two men who were sitting on baskets cutting cassava. The woman nodded. Both men were dressed in white loincloths, but one was wearing a feathered hat. The woman took me over to them and sat me down on a basket.

"Watch how they do it," she instructed.

"She's too young for the knife," the man with the feathered hat said. He looked at me with hard eyes. The other men went on cutting.

The woman gave me a bundle of branches and told me to cut the roots from them. She wasn't smiling now; her eyes were very solemn. I thought I'd angered her. I looked down at the ground.

"When they need more hands, they'll show you how to do it," she said.

"Take her over with the women," said the man in the feathered hat.

I didn't look at him. I cut the roots from the branches with shaking hands. He shoved a basket in front of me. I put the thick starchy roots in.

"When it is full, give it to me," he said.

I nodded, but didn't look up at him.

When I finally looked up, the woman who'd brought me there was over by the door getting ready to leave. The man in the striped pants touched her bare shoulder and she waited. And they stood talking. I couldn't hear what they were saying. I watched her long back, where the blouse fell from her shoulders almost to her waist. The man with the feathered cap slapped my fingers and pushed my head down.

"Mind what you are doing, girl," he said. "Here you will learn."

The other man looked up at him, but said nothing. I cut roots from the branches. I couldn't keep my fingers still. I didn't see when the woman left. I was afraid to ask when she would return. The man in the striped pants stood with his foot on a basket, watching us work.

I looked back at the man shielding his eyes from the fire, then I looked down at my work.

The Woman Whose Name She Does Not Know in the Beginning

When the long day was over, the woman who'd brought me there came for me. I followed her back to the place I'd first been taken. The house where she lived wasn't a part of the main house; it was some yards in the back of it, behind a clump of trees. It wasn't a hut but a square out-building made of plaster, although its floor was packed dirt like any other hut and its roof was made of thatch. The walls inside were clean and white and smooth and she had a little wooden dressing table and mirror. Another hammock was strung inside, a multi-colored hammock like her own.

"You'll sleep there," she said, "until you're used to the place, and then you'll sleep with the other women."

Her voice didn't seem to have the same kindness as it seemed to have before. Still I liked the straight way she stood, the way she stood with her head very high, as if she'd control of her own life, or took responsibility for it. I didn't think those thoughts in those days, though. I thought merely that she didn't stand like a slave, but like a free woman, like a senhora from the big house.

She went to the dresser and began to brush her hair, then she rubbed an oil into it, and into her face as well. There was the heavy smell of incense and coconut.

Not knowing what to do, I remained standing.

"Go on and sleep," she said kindly. "Aren't you tired? You're standing there like you're made of wood. Go on. You won't have long to rest, before I shake you in the morning."

I watched her oil her shoulders and breasts till they were glistening like her face and hair and bright eyes. Then I climbed into the hammock. My stomach growled and rumbled.

"You're hungry?" she said. "Didn't they feed you?"

"They gave me some cassava bread."

She reached under the dresser and came up with a bowlful of dried coconut which she handed to me. I took a handful.

"Here," she said, and gave the bowl to me.

I didn't know what to think of her. She moved so easily from a voice and show of kindness to one of anger and impatience, from soft eyes to fierce ones.

"When you're finished, put it on the dressing table....That's imported, from England. I'm going to sleep."

I started to tell her that I'd seen a woman from England who looked like a ghost with a red mouth and red cheeks, but she'd climbed into her hammock and turned her long back to me.

I finished half of the bowl of dried coconut meat and then tiptoed over to the dressing table. I set it down with a louder noise than I'd expected. I waited for her to complain, but she didn't. I went back and lay down in the hammock, picking little bits of coconut from my teeth.

"If I wasn't here, would you live here alone?" I asked, forgetting that she was a woman I didn't know.

She said nothing to me at first, so that I thought she must be sleeping, then she said, softly, with her back still to me, "Yes." Then there was silence. Then she said in an even softer voice, "Until a new young girl is purchased. First they are taken to Old Vera and then brought to me."

"Old Vera?"

"The old woman. Weren't you taken to the old woman first? The old woman? The healer? He always takes the new ones there first."

"No," I answered.

She said nothing. For a long time there was silence before she said into the silence and not to me, "Perhaps it's an ailment of spirit, then. Perhaps it's that."

I didn't know what she meant.

"Do you know of a place called Palmares?" I whispered.

She didn't answer at all.

I turned onto my stomach and soon fell asleep.

"Is that the girl?" I heard someone ask. "Is that her?"

"One of Father Tollinare's experiments," said another.

"And hasn't yet learned her proper place in the world."

I didn't know whether I was asleep or awake. But I fell asleep and I dreamed of Palmares, where one's true place in the world was said to be the same as any free man's or woman's.

Fazendo and the Indian Woman Who Was Not Touched by Mascarenhas

When my hammock began to move back and forth, I woke. It was morning. The woman was standing over me, her face solemn. She was holding a piece of fruit, what is called the mandacaru. I took it and thanked her. Without a word, she went to the mirror to brush her hair. It was very long and thick.

"Why do you brush your hair so much?" I asked, chewing the mandacaru. Again, I spoke to her as if she were not a stranger.

"Because I've got charms in my hair," she said with a smile. Her teeth were very white. Her face and shoulders were no longer shiny but very smooth.

I was silent.

"Haven't you heard that?" she asked. "About charms hidden in the hair?"

I shook my head.

She turned without smiling and said, "Come on."

I followed her to the place I'd been the day before, although today it seemed hotter, the heat from the furnace reaching even over where I sat, yards away. I sat down to cut roots, but there weren't any branches. Then I realized how strange it seemed, that branches had been picked as well as the roots. I sat watching the woman speak to the man in striped pants, then she left without saying a word to me. What would I do? I watched the woman at the furnace and the man shielding his eyes. I watched the woman standing over the round pot with her arms deep in cassava paste. Then the man in striped pants came over to me.

"I'm called Mascarenhas," he declared.

I said nothing.

"Do you know what these men are doing?" he asked.

I looked at the two men and the one in the feathered hat looked at me evilly, but continued cutting cassava even when his eyes were raised on mine.

"Yes," I said, looking back at Mascarenhas.

I didn't feel as shaky as I had the day before. I sat calmly. I tried to keep my eyes expressionless.

"Can you do what they're doing without making your hands bleed?"

"Yes, I can do it," I boasted and looked evilly at the man in the feathered hat, who returned the evil look, then I turned expressionless eyes to Mascarenhas. I said, "Yes," again, but the second time I wouldn't look at the man in the feathered hat.

Mascarenhas handed me a small knife. The man in the feathered hat began to laugh at this, then he was silent. I wouldn't look at him. He shoved a basket of cassava under my feet. I began to cut one without looking up at him. I wouldn't speak to him the next day nor the next, nor would he say a word to me, but when one of my baskets was finished, he'd shove another under my feet.

Three times a day, Indian women would enter carrying bundles of cassava. They were naked to the waist. One of the women I'd see sitting at the door of her hut with a small light-haired baby at her breast. Whenever this woman would enter, as silent as the other women, Mascarenhas would laugh and say in the woman's presence, "Me? I did not touch the Indian woman." She wouldn't look at him and always carried her head down.

I didn't know what this meant, but everyday the white man in the striped pants would say that. "Me? I did not touch the Indian woman." But I would see her sitting in front of her hut, her straight black hair against her shoulders, the baby sucking at her breast. I never heard her speak a word to anyone, not even to the other Indian women. I didn't realize then how strange it was, but there were no Indian men there, only women. Later I learned that the men refused to live there and were scattered in the forests; and at certain times certain ones would return to their women, and it was in that way children were conceived by them. I didn't know if this was true, because I'd only seen the Indian women there.

Of the Indian woman that Mascarenhas taunted, it was said, "She has forgotten her language and refuses to learn that of the masters." But I didn't feel she'd forgotten her own language. I felt that she simply refused to use either her own or that of the masters.

Each day I'd feel the man in the feathered cap looking at me with hard eyes, cutting his own cassava without looking at what he was doing.

After several days, he said, "I am called Fazendo." He looked at me coldly.

"I am Almedya," I replied, without turning my eyes to him. It was the first time I'd not put the "ita" on the end.

"Fazendo, she's too young for the knife," Mascarenhas said laughing. "I'm afraid she might bleed."

I looked at no one. I cut the cassava. I looked down at the ground. I carried my basket to the women when I'd finished. I didn't want my shoulders to be seen. I wanted to forget the language I had learned. I went back and sat silently, cutting cassava, until the woman entered and came and touched my shoulder. I started out with her still holding the little knife.

"Give that to me," Mascarenhas said. "I've told you always to give that to me."

I handed him the small knife and followed the woman.

The Wife of Martim Aprigio

I sat on the hammock and watched her brush her hair.

"Have you ever heard of a place called Palmares?" I dared to ask her again.

She turned and looked at me. She was very still. Her dark eyes looked fierce. Her hair was still swept back from the brushing. I felt afraid of her and yet I waited for her to speak. She began brushing her hair again, and climbed onto the hammock, still brushing it.

"I'm no longer a free woman because of that place," she said.

She stopped brushing and held the brush tightly in her lap.

"I thought women became free because of it," I said, watching her.

One side of her face remained still, while the other began to move, to twitch, the eye, the jawline.

"No, I'm no longer free because of it. But there are women there who're free as long as they stay there."

"Did you leave?"

"No. I was never at that place. I was free outside of it. I had my own house. I'd always been free. I was never a slave. Never. That's why even now I can hold my head as high as any woman. I was the wife of Martim Aprigio, a respected man, an engineer, and I was a respected woman, and we didn't always live in this country. After we were married, we lived in Holland for a long time. But after a while, Martim became like a crazy man and said a man wasn't free if he couldn't live anywhere. And so we came back here. But here we had to have papers to show our respectability. Martim Aprigio, a man who'd lectured in the Netherlands and Germany and England and France and at Russian courts, and who was even hired for projects by the Czar. That Martim Aprigio.

"But here, we always had to show our papers. Me, I got used to it. He didn't. The necessary papers and letters of introduction. In a wild country such as this, even noblemen carry letters of introduction. But free papers? No, he wouldn't get used to that.

"And then there was this man we helped, whom we gave food and drink. And it turned out that he was a spy for the escaped slaves at Palmares. They have their own spies, you see, everywhere. I didn't know it. I thought he too was a free man, a friend of my husband's, and I treated him with every kindness. But my husband knew who he was and what he was doing, and that a man could be executed for such a crime and a woman, and a woman captured and sold into slavery and..."

She did not go on. During her talk, she'd turned away from me, and it was only the still side of her face that I saw as she resumed her talk.

"He, Martim I mean, never told me how he came to be free and to be educated in foreign countries. He'd never tell me. But me? My mother was what they call 'a maker of angels,' an abortionist. All sorts of women came to her, even the wives of wealthy and important men. And there were enough of important men's wives. It's a horrible thing. When I was old enough to know what it was that got our freedom, why....No, I said nothing. I suppose anything to win one's freedom. But I walked about the house in silence, only silence." She turned to face me, both of her eyes very wide. "She stopped it, and began to sell angels. She sold little cakes that they call angels. And one day this black man, unlike any black man I'd ever seen in my whole life....He wore a dark suit, but he didn't wear it as some men, as if it didn't belong to him. It was his and his own life was his. I hadn't seen such a man ever, and I still haven't seen any.

"When my mother saw him coming, she'd pushed me up to the counter. I sold him a little angel, and he kept coming back and began to court me. He said he wouldn't be in this country long and wanted to marry me and take me with him. I didn't even know how he'd got to be the way he was, for he never told me, and then when we were in Holland, in Amsterdam, I saw the honor with which the people treated him. And it was not a false honor, not the false honor I saw him sometimes treated with here, when he'd show his letters of introduction. No, it was not a false honor, but real….

"He said he would be executed for such a crime. They took him one place and me another...But all my life I'd been protected from such evils as that and such evils as I've experienced here in this place. But I won't lower my head from it. I'll walk the same way that I did when I walked in the courtyards of noblemen."

She straightened her shoulders and began to brush her hair very hard. I stared at her high smooth forehead.

The next day I learned the difference between the sweet cassava and the bitter cassava. Wine was made from the juice of the sweet cassava, and bread from the starchy root. The juice of the bitter cassava was poison and every bit of it must be squeezed and baked out. Cassava branches were cut and then replanted for new cassava plants. If the branch of a cassava plant were cut and the roots were kept in the ground, the cassava root would stay whole and good and could be dug up many years later and eaten. I learned to make war flour by toasting dry cassava. War flour would last for a year, but fresh cassava flour would only last for two days.

Dream of Feathers

The wife of Martim Aprigio soon sent me to live with the old woman and the rest of the women who worked at the cassava barn. They lived in a very large hut with rows of hammocks. Although they never spoke of her, I felt the distance there seemed between them and this woman who once had been free. I also wondered what it was she did besides provide a place for the new women (I called myself a woman then) to stay.

I only remember her taking me to the cassava barn in the mornings. And I learned that she was the only black woman who would stand speaking to Mascarenhas. The others met him with silence, although he'd speak to them freely, that is when he didn't think that they were working properly or fast enough. Mascarenhas's skin was a dark red, even though he was a white man, or considered himself to be one. It looked as if it had been baked over the furnace like the cassava bread.

Now I came and went with the rest of the women. It was said to be a large plantation, although it was only a corner of it that I saw, and didn't feel I could roam freely as I had at Entralgo's place. In fact, here I'd not even seen the master and learned that the man who'd purchased me was not the master but a man named Sobrieski, a Polish shoemaker who sometimes acted as the master's agent, and who did most of his business from the master, whose name was Azevedo, but of whom no one ever spoke. No one had ever taken an order from him directly, and he stayed, as far as I could tell, within the thick walls of his mansion and when he ventured outside, he was carried around in a curtained hammock. Although I'd heard that some masters would have their slaves carry them about, I'd not grown up with that, as Entralgo strolled about his plantation freely, giving orders and punishments, riding his horse through his canefields and orchards. It was only the women who he kept sheltered, and it was said that he'd whipped one of his daughters almost to death for letting a stranger see her standing at the window. The girl had only been three or four, and it was said that there were still scars on her body, and they said that he would regret it later when it came time for her to marry, for it would lessen her price. At first, I hadn't understood it, when they used the word "price," since the daughters of Entralgo were free.

"Who is that pacha?" I asked, the first time I saw the curtained hammock.

A group of women were crowded in the doorway watching.

"Pacha?" asked one of the women. "That's the master himself."

"What is his name?"

"Azevedo it is."

"Has no one ever seen him?"

"The old woman Vera has seen him."

"The old woman has seen everybody."

"Yes, even when he comes out into the yard he rides in a covered hammock."

"I saw his hand once. He was eating grapes and he threw a handful of seeds out from behind the curtain. A very delicate hand too."

"Does he have a wife and children?" I asked.

"No, Vera says he doesn't," one of the women said.

I wondered if I'd ever see him. Vera came to the doorway and there was no more talk of Azevedo. I wondered why none of the women were ever with any of the men I'd seen, for on the Entralgo plantation one often saw men and women together. But I'd only seen three men afterall. There were the two men who cut cassava, and the one who threw coal into the furnace. I asked one of the women about this. She said nothing at first. In fact, it was many days before she answered my question. We were returning at night from the cassava barn and I was walking alone. She left the other women, came back and walked with me.

"There's something wrong with all the women who work on this part of the plantation," she whispered.

I said that there was nothing wrong with me and tried to hold my head as high as the wife of Martim Aprigio.

"We're none of us able to have children," she explained. "It's either from mutilation or nature or age."

I was silent, then I looked at her.

"My reason is the first one," she said solemnly. "But I won't tell the story. It's a horror and I refuse to tell horrors to anyone. There are enough of those in this wicked world."

I said nothing. I noticed how small the steps were she took, as we walked behind the other women. She had a very tall and slender body and she stooped to enter the low door of the hut when we arrived there. As soon as we were inside, she raised herself onto her hammock and closed her eyes.

"Almeydita."

I'd not been called Almeydita for a very long time. I turned and the old woman Vera was looking at me. "I hear you've dreams to tell," she said.

I'd told no one of the dreams and daydreams I used to have. In fact, I'd had no daydreams here.

"I'm the one you come to if you've dreams to tell," she said, then she climbed into her hammock and slept.

I climbed into my hammock and went to sleep and dreamed.

In the morning, a Sunday, I followed her into a low doorway. There was the smell of wood burning. She said that white men were in the forest making a canoe. I started to say that the smell came from inside the place she'd brought me to, but she looked at me, and I did not speak. She sat on a mat and gently pulled me down beside her.

"Almeydita," she called the old name again.

I looked at the gray in her hair and the gold rings in her ears. There were small brown specks in her eyes. Her cheekbones were high and her eyes were like almonds. There were wrinkles in the corners of her eyes and on her forehead. She looked at me with her lips pressed together, then she smiled.

"Tell me your dreams," she said. She was solemn again.

"Is Vera your real name?" I asked.

She raised her eyebrows and made the wrinkles in her forehead deeper.

"And what does the real name of this woman have to do with you?" she asked.

"Because someone told me that your name was not your own."

"Is anyone's?" she asked.

She felt the upper part of my arm for no reason I could see, except that it was very thin, then she removed her hand.

"And will you refuse to tell me the dream without the name?" she said, and smiled.

"No," I replied. "They were wearing feathers on their heads and blowing horns."

"Who?"

"Black men. Pretos. They came down from the top of the mountain on two sides and they were wearing white trousers and no shirts and their heads were full of feathers. Some had feathers on their hats like the white men and others had bands around their heads and feathers sticking out of their bands. There was so much noise and shouting. Some were beating drums, some were blowing horns, some were playing flutes and trumpets. They had swords and bows and arrows, torches, axes."

"Were there rifles?"

"No. Not even the white men. The white men had swords too."

I stopped and looked at her. She nodded for me to go on.

"On the top of the hill there was a fence surrounding it made of wood with sharp points. I only saw part of the fence. I couldn't see what it was surrounding. But the men. All these men coming down from both sides of the mountain. They were preparing for a great battle it seemed. The white men were afraid and turned back."

"What was certain?"

"What do you mean?"

"Which men were certain?"

"I don't know what you mean."

She didn't explain. She stood and pulled me up.

"As long as you're here, you must tell your dreams to me."

She had branches on her head and flowers. Flowers and leaves on the branches. A branch on each side of her head. Two bands wrapped around her head to hold the branches, and she was wearing a wide necklace with many colors. She'd grown into a young beautiful woman dressed this way, and there were moons painted between her breasts. Painted with red paint, red moons facing each other. And her breasts were large. I'd never seen breasts so large. The breasts were large and there was a big space between them that the red moons filled. She wore bracelets on the upper parts of her arms, and there were little branches hanging from the bracelets. These branches had leaves but no flowers. And her eyes, her eyes were bright and looked as if they were slanted all the way up to the sky.

"You've not forsaken the principles of your religion," she said.

I didn't understand her. It was dream language that I didn't understand. She took my arm and we sat down on the ground again. She was old Vera again.

"You're a woman," she said to me softly.

Then she wasn't there and I was sitting in the doorway of a house that wasn't my own. There were red lines on my forehead and cheekbones. I was within myself and outside as well. I was weaving something. A blanket? Yes, I was weaving a blanket with many colors in it. My shoulders were round and not sharp and awkward and angular. My breasts were round. I was wearing a wide necklace and bracelets on my arms. I was wearing earrings and my eyes were painted, dark lines around them. There were two baskets and a big shell for cigarette smoke, but I was not smoking. There was a guitar and a mandolin hanging in the doorway. I looked up at a man who was carrying a sheaf of arrows, a very tall man. We were not talking. I watched him remove his jacket.

"Now you're dreaming the dream of a woman," she said, an old woman standing in front of me, touching my upper arm.

I said nothing.

"Grandmother," I whispered. "Is this the negro asylum?"

"It is Ituiba," she said quietly.

"What?" I asked.

"My real name. It is Ituiba," she said. "That's my real name, not Vera. Come."

I followed her outside where there were white men carving a canoe. It was the morning of the next day and I followed her into the cassava barn. I kept waiting to grow tired, but I felt through the day as if I'd rested the whole night.

An Obsessed Man

One day I saw the covered hammock. Two men carried it tied to a long pole, and there was a heavy rug of some kind slung over it, so that it covered him completely, and I wondered how he breathed, as I could not see the slit on one side. It left from the back of the mansion and traveled down to the little thatched house where I'd first stayed. Then it couldn't have been but five or ten minutes before the hammock came out again. I'd felt faint and Vera had asked Mascarenhas to let me stand in the yard. When the hammock left the little house, the men who carried it walked a few yards, and then stopped as if someone inside had commanded them to, although I, at a little distance from them, had heard no one. Then the men continued and carried the hammock into the back of the house.

I'd not been back inside for very long when Sobrieski came inside the cassava barn and said something to Mascarenhas. Then it was Mascarenhas who came to me and told me to go with Sobrieski. I handed him my knife and followed the slender and silent Polish shoemaker. It was into the back of the mansion that he took me, and through a long corridor.

The master sat on a hammock. There were ruffles around his collar and ruffles that hung from the sleeves of his dressing gown. Sobrieski left, closing the door. I stood in the center of the room and stared at hands that were as plump as sausages but as delicate as lace. His dark gray eyes were sunken in puffy jaws. He kept staring at me.

"Why do you look at me with your strange eyes?" he asked.

I didn't answer. I was barefoot, and there was still cassava juice on my hands and dress and feet.

"Why do you look at me so strangely with those eyes? Come nearer."

I walked nearer, but was still not very close to him in the long room.

"Why do you look at me so?"

I was still silent.

"I've not had a woman in this room for a very long time. I'm not a common man, you know. I'm a strange man, an unusual man."

I still stood watching him.

"I haven't dined with a woman in a long time," he said.

I kept looking at him, his jaws and fingers uncooked sausages, his eyes hidden in his face. He called out a name that sounded like Pita and one of the men who'd carried his hammock entered and stood very stiffly, waiting for orders.

"Bring ham, coconut milk, sugar loaf, rice, pears, biscuits, wine, ah fish," he said. "And tell Sobrieski I want him to fit the woman for a pair of shoes. Sandals. Any other kind will be difficult for her now. Have you ever worn shoes? Didn't Father Tollinare ever put shoes on his little experiments?"

I shook my head.

"Sandals for now," said Azevedo.

The man nodded and went out. He didn't look at me at all. I remember only the wife of Aprigio had been wearing shoes--sandals. But I'm sure she hadn't been barefoot in the courtyards of noblemen.

"A man should be with a good woman every now and then," he said.

At first it had been curiosity that made me stare at him so, for I'd thought all masters were as lean and well-proportioned as Entralgo. Now I stared at him in fear.

"Sit down," he said. "It's been a long time since I've had a woman to look at me like that. Your eyes are lovely, my dear."

He pointed to one of the many mats and huge many-colored pillows on the floor of the room. I remained standing.

"I'm not a common man, you know," he repeated. "I'm an unusual man. I've kept to myself my whole life until now, not even servants in the house, no servants in the house, not a woman. I cleared all this ground myself, no help none, a man all alone, and planted the first cassava, sugar cane, bananas. No slaves for me. I built this house for myself, no help, by myself, all by myself. I'm not a usual man. You look at me now, eh? Well, I wasn't the same man you're staring at now, my dear, being carried about. No. And hiding from people? Well, they'd have hidden from me. But there was no one here but me then. Nobody. A man alone. I built this house by myself, cleared the forest. You're not looking at a usual man, my dear. Sit down."

I remained standing.

"I built all these grounds with my own hands."

He waved his hands in the air. I couldn't imagine him building anything with them.

"You're not looking at the same man," he said. "It was only after it was done, after everything was built, that you people came here. It was only after I got to be an old man that I needed servants in the house. And no woman. I didn't need a woman here at all, not even a Tupi, and haven't dined with a good woman in many years."

Pita entered carrying a long tray which he set on the floor. He left and came back with another long tray full of all the things that Azevedo had ordered him to bring. Plta left again, and returned with another man. Together they arranged the long cushions and then lowered Azevedo's hammock to the floor. They placed a mat and pillows for me, but I remained standing. This time Pita looked at me, and looked away.

"Sit down," Azevedo said to me.

Pita glanced at me again.

"Come, my woman," Azevedo said, waving his hands across the tray of food.

I remained standing. Pita looked at me and kept his eyes on me. I went to the pillows that had been laid for me and sat down across from Azevedo.

"I'm done with you. I don't need anyone else," Azevedo said, and Pita and the other man left, closing the door.

Azevedo sat looking at me, then he waved his hand across the trays again. "Take what you want, my dear."

I took nothing. I still stared at him, at his small gray eyes. He reached down and picked up a piece of smoked fish and held it out to me. He kept holding it out. Although I didn't take it, he wouldn't put it down. There was something in his face that made me feel as if I should take it, but I couldn't. He still held it out.

"I am not a common man," he said. "You're not looking at the man I was then. If you were looking at the man I was then, you'd not refuse me, not even you."

I suddenly reached out and took it. He smiled and reached down for another piece. He ate it in small quick bites. I held mine in my hand for a long time, and then ate it slowly. He held out other things to me, which I took. I'd never had so much food at one time, though I'd often seen the masters eat like that. Some things on the tray I'd never eaten before, and some things I'd never even seen before. I took what he handed to me until my stomach began to feel strange, and I held it. I wondered how the masters ate like that without their stomachs complaining.

"What's wrong?" he asked.

"I'm not used to eating so much."

"Mascarennas doesn't feed you?" he asked.

"Yes, but it's mostly the same things again and again. Cassava bread and cassava pudding."

He handed me a bowl of coconut milk.

"Here, drink this. It will help," he said.

I took it and drank and set the bowl back down on the tray. Then I wouldn't speak again. I sat very still and wouldn't speak or look at him. I felt ashamed for eating with him.

"Now you are fed, you would deny me."

I pretended not to know what he meant. Perhaps I didn't know. I wouldn't look at him. My stomach felt very unsettled, and I held it. I wasn't sure whether it was the shame or the food that unsettled it.

"Look at me. I want to see your lovely eyes."

I looked at him. He put his hand under his coat and kept looking at me.

"I am not a usual man," he said slowly. "Why are you watching me with such eyes? Speak to me. Say something. This isn't an ordinary man that you're looking at. No. I came to this place alone and cleared the land by myself."

He stared at me with gray eyes deep inside his face. His hand moved back and forth and up and down inside his long coat.

"I came here alone and built this house for myself and alone, see how thick the walls are and how cool it is inside, it's as big and good as any you've seen, alone, with nobody, I cleared and planted, a man alone, ah yes, I didn't need a woman here, no, I didn't need a woman in this place, ah yes, why are you looking at me with such lovely eyes?"

He kept his hand inside his coat and rose up slightly. Then he settled down in the hammock, and seemed to sigh. His gray eyes got wider, and looked at me fully.

"You're like a woman who never moves. You never move and have stopped speaking. Are you of flesh and blood?"

Suddenly, there was a knock at the door and Sobrieski said his name. Azevedo told him to enter. He came in and bowed to Azevedo, then began, without a word, to measure my feet for sandals. Then he left quickly without a word. He had light-colored flat hair, and was dressed in a white shirt and trousers more like a slave's than a master's, although the first time I'd seen him he'd worn expensive looking clothes, and I'd been certain he was my new master.

"The leatherworker claims he's some kin to me," Azevedo said with a smirk. "That we're brothers by a different father but the same woman." He laughed out loud. "We're all brothers by the same father. Ha Ha Ha Ha. Aren't we all?" He paused. "Speak to me." He waited. "Is your stomach still unsettled?"

I didn't answer. He'd taken his hand from his coat and wiped it on a cloth. Now he put it back inside. "Speak to me," he whispered. His eyes looked pleading. Then he stared out, expressionless. "You think I'm an ordinary man. But you're looking at what I am now. Ask the old woman, ask Old Vera. Ask her what this man was then and that's what she'll remember, all she'll remember, because I haven't let her get a glimpse of me in years and so that's all she'll remember, because that's all she's seen. Ask her what I'm like, my dear, and she won't speak to you of the man you're looking at, because she's never seen this one." His hand went back and forth. "I built it by myself and I kept it, and then her with her slanted eyes, no, not like now, huge almond eyes, and her breasts like sweet cassava. In those days, mind you, I could eat cassava all the time. Old Vera. But it's the same as me. All you see now is the old woman, afraid to show her bosom, but then, in those days she was too handsome, too handsome. I never needed any woman, and then I never needed any other woman."

I stared at him and started to rise, but he waved his other hand at me while the one inside his coat moved up and down, then back and forth.

"When I first brought her here I had flowers everywhere, everywhere. And she'd put them all over. She'd put them all over her body, on her arms, around her ankles, around her head, flowers, banana leaves, cassava branches."

I looked at him, my eyes wide, for he was describing the woman I had seen.

"She wasn't afraid of her bosom then. Sweet, ripe, cassava. She was too handsome. And I was no ordinary man myself then. You look at me now, but you don't remember what she remembers. When I first came here, I worked like a slave myself, a slave and more, cleared my own land, and built this house. I went for years without the touch of a woman. No, you're not looking at the same man she remembers." He stopped moving his hand and stared at me, then he began to move it again. He raised himself up and seemed to stay there, almost floating atop his hammock, his hand still inside his long coat.

"She said that it was I who made cruelty here. That it was I who made it, as if it didn't already exist in the world. I who made it….There's a code of silence between us now. But she'll know. She'll know that I"ve been with a good woman. She'll know it. She has her ways of knowing such things." His whole body seemed to settle again.

He removed his hand from his coat and wiped it on the cloth.

"What did you do?" I asked.

"What?" He spoke quickly.

"What cruelty to her? What did you do to her?"

"Cruelty? Me? What did I do to her? It's what she did to me is more the question."

He sat and stared at me. He put his hand in his coat, then removed it and wiped it on the cloth again. He looked at me for a very long time. He raised himself up again, in anger, I thought, then he peered at me calmly.

"I brought her bottles of red wine from Europe. I had a gold necklace sent over, a wide gold necklace that had once belonged to an Egyptian princess, or could've belonged to one. She claimed she was lararaca--is that the name of it?--the great magic serpent, the mystical serpent. She said yes she was one." He stared at his hand as if it were lararaca, and then he wiped it on the cloth again."I treated her like a lady, but I should've known what she was from the beginning, and what she'd do when she had her chance to do it."

"What did she do?" I asked.

"Destroy. She tried to destroy everything. All I'd built. Everything."

"Burn it?" I asked, thinking of my grandmother.

"Burn? What do you mean burn? Did she tell you? Did she betray me in that too? A code of silence we had."

"No, she didn't tell me."

"Are you another lararaca? I won't put up with it."

I shook my head.

"Burn?" he asked. "She tried to burn. Burn all the grounds, cotton, sugar cane, cassava, banana trees. And to burn this, to burn this." I thought he would put his hand in his long coat again, but he waved it in the air. "She tried to burn this mansion with me inside of it. Burn it while I was right here inside. Burn it to the ground. My cruelty? Ah, and now she's afraid of her own bosom. Why do I tell you all this?" He peered at me. "Did she send you here? I've not had a woman in this house. Did she send you here?"

"No, you did, Sir. You sent for me."

"Cruelty? I'm not the one who brought cruelty. I left her for dead. I walked away from her. But she healed miraculously. Plants she knows, herbs, her magic," he said with contempt. "Or maybe she is the old great lararaca. But it wasn't my cruelty, not mine. Did she tell you it was mine?"

I shook my head.

"She healed miraculously, and so we have a code of silence, and the old serpent doesn't enter here. I've watched her grow old, but me, all she remembers is the man bending over her with the machete and what pain she felt, if lararaca is capable of that. But that's the man she remembers, and I've kept it so. But her. Does lararaca grow old? I left her for dead, laying against the house she tried to burn, with me inside. But I came out in time, and saw what the witch was doing. And we've a code of silence, and she doesn't know of the man you're seeing now. She only remembers that one....Did she send you here to spy on me?"

"You sent for me, Sir."

He looked at me and wiped his hand across his chest as if he were slashing with a machete. I've heard of such sexual punishment for women, and my grandmother had said that she'd seen it done, the breasts of an unfortunate woman cut off. It was whispered that Entralgo had once tried to do the same thing to Antonia but that Father Tollinare had forbidden it.

"The man was drunk and angry at someone and the woman got in his way, and so he cut her breasts off. There wasn't any crime she'd done."

My grandmother had told me that story when my mother was away, because my mother didn't like her to tell me such stories.

"She won't always live in this little world," my grandmother had replied. "They're not all Entralgos. There are Corricaos too."

Yes, that was the first time I'd remembered hearing the name of the slave breeder Corricao. It was said that he bred even his own daughters and the daughters of his daughters, but I'd never seen him. But whenever grandmother told such stories or mentioned the names of such masters as that one, my mother would look at her with anger and had even once said, referring to my grandmother's insanity, "And maybe she'll not always be sane, but she is now, and I want to keep her that way as long as I can."

My grandmother had said nothing then. I looked at her and smiled and made her smile too.

"My cruelty?" Azevedo was still asking when I emerged from my reverie. "It's only that I didn't recognize the serpent in the woman. That was my error. But I won't make that error again." He flung his hand into the air. "But she'll see. She'll see I've been with a good woman again. You're not as handsome as her though."

His head settled against his heavy neck and he fell asleep. I sat there for several hours, it seemed, until he woke and ignoring me asked Pita to go for Sobrieski to take me back.

When I entered the hut, it was the old woman's eyes that stared at me without stopping. Had he been right? Had she made use of me to see him for herself. It was rumored that witches could do that, use the eyes of others to see whatever and whoever they wanted to see. Had I seen everything she'd wanted me to see? Had I heard more than she'd wanted? Thinking she had, had he broken their code of silence?

I kept waiting for her to say something to me, but she never did, except there were times when she would stare at me for a very long time. I wouldn't look at her at those times, and when I did look my eyes would not go beyond her flat and covered bosom.

New Sandals

The next morning when I came to work, new sandals had been left beside my stool. I left them sitting there and didn't try them on. Fazendo, one of the men who cut cassava, continued to look at me evilly through the day. The Indians entered as usual to bring bushels of cassava, and when a certain woman entered, Mascarenhas, as usual, would say, "Me? I didn't touch the Indian woman" except this time he added, "Me? I'm not the one. I didn't make a present of new sandals."

I said nothing, but I felt shame again, although nothing had occurred between the master and myself. I stared ahead of me, and nodded when the woman set the basket of ripe cassava by my feet. This time I looked up at her. Her eyes were not staring blankly as they usually did, she was staring straight at me, her flat long hair hanging down on all sides. I didn't know what to make of her expression, and glanced quickly away from her.

"Me? I didn't touch the Indian woman. You think I'm the one? I didn't make a present of new sandals either."

I glanced at him expecting him to be looking at me, but he wasn't. He was staring straight ahead, standing in the center of the cassava barn, with a long whip I hadn't as yet seen him use.

I felt Fazendo's eyes on me, but didn't dare look at him. I wondered if the same were true of the men as I'd been told of the women who worked there. There were only three men among us, and the two servants of Azevedo that I'd seen. Azevedo had called me one of Father Tollinare's experiments, but did he have his own cruel experiments?

When the day was over I dropped my little knife beside my basket. I looked at the sandals and started to leave them there. I sensed Fazendo waiting to see what I would do. I lifted them up quickly by the leather straps, not knowing why I'd done so, and left, walking behind the other women.

"Me? I'm not the one…"

I imagined his sly eyes on me. Outside, Fazendo's hand slid against my arm. I didn't look at him, although I let him walk beside me.

"Do you stay now with those women?" he asked.

"Yes."

"You don't know if the shoes fit."

I looked at him. He wasn't watching me, but looking ahead. I stared at the smooth line of his jaw and his thick hair.

"So you've seen him," he said. "So you know what he looks like."

"I've seen only as much of him as you."

His eyes narrowed at me. "He'll send for you again. He'll send for you anytime."

"There won't be any other time," I snorted. "I'll escape and go to Palmares where I'll be a free woman."

He laughed, but looked at me strangely. "Who told you about that place? What do you know of that place?"

"No one told me. I'll be a free woman and no one can touch me there."

He laughed again. "Oh, there'll be plenty to touch you there, my dear."

I frowned.

"If I wanted you for myself," he said, "why I'd go to Mascarenhas. But you've nothing. You've nothing for a real man."

"And isn't he real?"

"Who, Mascarenhas? I have my doubts."

"No, the master." I pointed to the mansion. "Isn't he real?"

"You're the one who's seen him. But I have my doubts about that one too."

Then he stopped walking. I stopped a moment, but seeing he had nothing else to say to me and had meant for me to go on, I continued. When I got to the door of the women's hut, I looked back and saw him waiting. Then he turned quickly and I entered the long hut. The old woman Vera's eyes were on me as I set the sandals on the ground, and climbed into my hammock. She looked at the sandals as though she would burn them.

The Stranger

A strange white man came riding into Azevedo's plantation. He was riding a skinny, pointy-eared horse, and there was an umbrella over his head. Everyone else after looking at him went about their business, but me I stood and watched the strange skinny man on the skinny horse. The Indian woman who spoke to no one was sitting in her doorway holding the light-haired baby on her lap. The man kept looking around at people. He looked at me. It was Sunday and I too sat outside my hut, weaving and reweaving and reweaving the same basket. He rode straight to the Indian woman and got down from the skinny horse. His own face was very long like the animal's, and sallow. He got down from the horse, folded his umbrella, and knelt in front of her on one knee.

"My mistress, my lady," he said. "Don't' you appreciate the aspect of a man of good character who would live his whole life in your honor?"

She continued to watch him but said nothing.

"Who would protect you from any danger and just now has traveled a long and treacherous journey to come to you."

I heard a few suppressed giggles while others went about their business, weaving or carving, or other of their own work they spent the holiday doing. Even Old Xavier, who was known as the wizard and was Old Vera's rival on the plantation (those who were not satisfied with Old Vera's cures would go to Arraial Xavier and vice versa), had brought out his small bottles of tonics and was exchanging one for a bag of ground nuts a broad-shouldered man was handing to him. He too acted as though the stranger were not there, continuing to examine his bottles, to taste samples which could cure everything from maculo (diarrhea), to the "white man's disease," and there were some bottles that were for love-sorcery, to cure what Xavier called "diseases of the heart"; he even boasted of having medicines to cure soul ailments.

Watching Old Xavier, I'd lost the beginning of what the stranger said, but heard only the words "perpetual adoration" as he continued on his bent knee. Then before he stood he reached for the woman's hand and gently kissed the back of it. She allowed him to, and then returned her hand to hold the baby more securely.

Suddenly, I couldn't tell whether the man was Portuguese or Indian or Negro, and the hat he was wearing didn't allow one to see the texture of his hair. He said nothing else to the woman, but rose in silence, got upon his horse and rode away the same way he'd come. The woman remained sitting as if nothing unusual had happened.

I was the only one who continued to watch her. For a moment, I was uncertain whether this was one of my waking dreams or whether it had actually happened. And I had become afraid to ask questions of the old woman Vera, because she continued to look at me strangely, and had not said one word to me since I'd been sent for by Azevedo. So I kept looking at the Indian woman until the baby pulled at her breasts and began to suck, then I went over to her rival, the old man Xavier, whom I discovered was also the cook for Azevedo, because he spoke Portuguese well and knew something of the Christian religion, which Azevedo expected of his house servants and those who touched his food, no matter what "sorcery" they used outside or what concoctions they made for others.

I walked up to him and stood there for a long time without speaking. I'd never spoken to him and was a little afraid. He had a very long neck that looked like a goose's neck. As I stood there, he squatted on the ground and drew my eyes, then he stood up.

"Do you wish to speak to me or to the one who touches the eyes without medicines and heals them? If you wish to speak to me, then you must translate your silence into words. Come on, what is it?"

"I came to ask about that man."

"Haven't you seen a lunatic before?" He tasted from one of his bottles, squinted his eyes, and tasted again. "He's a lunatic, that's all."

"Who is he, where does he come from? I haven't seen him anywhere before or anyone like him."

"Are you sure of that?" He squinted at me. "He's a traveling lunatic. You've heard of troubadours, haven't you?"

I nodded.

"Well, he's something like that, except he's a traveling crazy man. Who knows where he's been? But he certainly comes here twelve times a year to make much ado over that woman. Twelve times a year he brings himself into her presence. Don't ask me what it's for. I accept the gifts that've been given me, and sometimes the spirits enter me and I can see the future and the past, but otherwise I'm a rational man. I'll tell you what he thinks he sees in her. He thinks her eyes reflect the universe. Ha. The universe, mind you. He thinks her right eye's the sun and her left eye's the moon. What do you think of that?"

I watched the woman staring down at the child.

"As for me," said Xavier, "I don't see the universe in any woman. And if I did see it, I wouldn't believe my own eyes." He lifted one of his bottles and smelled it, put a bit on his finger and tasted it. "Well, I'll say one thing, he's a free man, and that's more than I can say for myself. I'm not Old

Vera I'm not, who claims she's free when the soul of one of the gods enters. Me, I'm a rational man."

He screwed on the top of one of the bottles and handed it to me.

"What's this?" I asked.

"An antidote," he said. "I'm a love-sorcerer, am I not? You're the one to decide what it's for and when it will be useful."

He handed the bottle to me in one hand and held out the other one. I wondered again whether the man had been real or all in my imagination. I knew that if he hadn't appeared I would have never dared to say a word to Old Xavier.

I handed him the basket I had woven and rewoven many times.

I stared at the black liquid in the bottle. It reminded me of what my mother had made from the black root and had given me to drink. I took the bottle and looked again at the Indian woman who sat calmly in the door with her fair-haired baby.

"Maybe he's not crazy," said Xavier, looking at the woman. "But me? I haven't seen the universe in any women's eyes and don't intend to."

I went back and sat in front of the squat, long building, imagining it was myself the lunatic had come and knelt before, seeing the universe in my eyes.

The Hidden Woman

I don't know if it was Old Vera's machinations (because I had seen Azevedo or had dared to seek out the advice of her rival Old Xavier) or whether it was an idea the master had his own self, but I was rented to a woman in the city, and it was at that time that I realized that I was destined to meet people who were repetitions and variations of my grandmother. Sometimes when I met them I wondered whether they were indeed my grandmother, capable of doing what they said witches in the Old Country could do, transform themselves. Witches in the Old Country, they said, were capable of all sorts of transformations and transmutations. But I don't know if any of that is true. The woman herself had come for me driving the wagon and wearing a man's trousers, shirt, and hat. At first I hadn't recognized the woman as a woman, for she sat silently in the driver's seat and I on straw in the back of the wagon, although I noticed that there was a certain strangeness to the curve of the man's back. She'd covered her hair with a huge straw hat as I'd seen many wear in that country. As we journeyed into town, she never said a word to me.

We entered the wide gray streets of the city and drove around the back of the little shop. How the woman had rented me from Azevedo I never knew, as he kept himself hidden from strangers as well as most of his servants, and he seemed, as we saw no strangers enter or leave the mansion, to have no friends among the townspeople or other plantation owners in the region. I assume, though, that Sobrieski must have acted as his agent in this as other matters.

At the rear of the shop we stopped and the man, the woman whom I thought was a man then, jumped down. At the time I didn't know that there would be such another scene sometime in my life, but for quite a different purpose from my going to serve someone. I don't mean to jump ahead in my story but only to point to my suspicions of Old Vera's or perhaps even my own grandmother's machinations in this destiny. Nevertheless, the woman, acting as a man, helped me down, but still didn't speak to me, and then she opened the heavy gray door and went into the back room of the shop, which looked to be a shop where women's hats were sold.

The man said, "Wait here."

I waited, as the man went into another small room. I remained standing. There was a rosewood table and two hard rosewood benches on either side of it on the left side of a curtained door leading to the front. A very tall dark mahogany chest of drawers which ended only a few inches below the ceiling stood beside the table. There were two rosewood hard chairs against the wall. On the left wall was a slender hammock.

A woman who seemed to be in her early thirties came out, dressed in a plainly cut silk dress. She resembled the man and I thought she must be his sister. She had in her hand the hat he'd been wearing. I thought she must be a special servant to the hatmaker who'd hired me to work for her.

"What does your mistress want me to do?" I inquired.

She began to laugh. Her teeth were very white and her smile made her somewhat pretty, but the solemn expression she returned to me made her a plain-looking dark yellow skinned woman.

I looked at her, my expression a curious frown. I could see no one in the back room, although she'd left the door wide open. There was cloth, straw, feathers scattered about on low gray benches, but I could see no one.

"Where did your brother go?"

She laughed again and was as quietly solemn. I stared at her, thinking surely this too was a crazy woman.

"He's not my brother. But he appears and disappears when I wish him to. He makes life easier for me sometimes, other times more difficult. But he went for you more easily than I could have, carrying a note from our mistress."

I caught the funny way she'd said the last thing and kept my curious expression. I arched an eyebrow and stared at the hair about her shoulders, the thick fuzziness of a black woman, the flatness and looseness of a white's combined. I thought of a story I'd heard about a magic man in a lamp.

"How can a real man appear and disappear?" I asked.

"Did I say he was a real man?"

Yes, she was certainly crazy, I thought, for I'd surely seen him with my own eyes, although it was true he'd not spoken one word to me. I wondered whether mulattoes were sent to the negro asylum or whether they had their own asylum, like the whites. She laughed and pushed her long hair up and put the hat back on. *She* was the man. I began to laugh.

"So your mistress has only one servant and she uses you for a woman and a man," I said, feeling that I'd caught the joke and I clapped my hands, though softly, afraid the mistress might hear.

She was not delighted at all. She frowned and looked more solemn. She removed the hat and shook her hair out.

"I'm your mistress," she said. "I'm your mistress and the man."

I shook my head. "No," I said. "I don't like such jokes. You're a colored woman. There aren't any colored women mistresses." Then I was doubtful, as I thought of the strange colored woman I'd seen once before, the captain's wife. Then I added, "I've never had a colored woman for a mistress."

"Well, I'm to be," she said. "At least until the festival is over."

I looked down at the hard wooden floor and my bare feet. I still wouldn't wear the sandals, though I'd not thrown them away, keeping them on the floor when I slept and in my hammock during the day, and listening daily to Mascarenhas talk of the gift of sandals he'd not given as well as the flesh and blood gift that had not been his.

"Well, they're having themselves a parade to celebrate their Indian ancestry. Suddenly all the people in this town have got Indian grandmothers and great grandmothers and so forth and they're celebrating them. Changing their names to Indian names, but it's just their Christian names and their mother's names they're changing, the rascals, for it's their father's name that holds the prestige for them. Do you think they'd change their prestige names?" She asked this question strangely, paused, but didn't look as if she expected me to answer, then went on, "The only Indian names any of them know are the names for trees and rivers." She laughed. "So they're all naming themselves after trees and rivers. And the mayor's declaring it a special holiday, and there'll be parades and dances, and as for me, I've been commissioned to make special hats and headgear for the devils to look just like those Indians wear. And so that's why I needed extra help."

My mouth fell open. I'd never heard brancos referred to as devils and rascals before.

"Why didn't you get an Indian woman?" I asked.

"I've got sketches of what I want. I wanted someone who made things, wove baskets and of some ability, and you were the one they sent. Anyway, they kept telling me that their Indian women didn't make good servants." She tossed her hat into one of the chairs. "Does it surprise you I'm your mistress and a free colored woman?"

I nodded. "Does the town know you? Do you fool them too?"

"The town knows me, and I've no problems here. None to speak of. My father was a carpenter and built the church and many of its ornaments. He was a respected man here. Commissioned to build a lot of the better houses."

"A free colored man?"

"No," she replied, as if angered that I'd think so. "A white man, a Portuguese carpenter, and my mother was his slave." She sounded impatient. "She was his slave and he freed her and me. There's a lot we have to do. Come on."

She started into the small room and when I didn't follow her she turned and looked at me meanly.

"Come on, I said. Do you think that because I'm a colored woman I don't have the right to give orders or that I won't punish you if you don't obey them?" She stood with her arms folded, her large eyes narrow.

As she turned again to enter the small room, I followed her.

My first task was to dye all the white hen feathers yellow. The peacock feathers and all the other splendid ones from parrots and macaws I was to leave as they were. I worked at a low bench with bowls of yellow, red and green dye, while she sat at a high table with parchment spread in front of her on which were certain symbols and designs. I don't know if they had any meaning; most were abstract, although one looked like a running deer. They were designs she had seen, she explained, from Indian art, sculpture, and headdresses.

At first she'd said she'd seen them, and then she clarified that she'd copied them from a Jesuit's library. She explained that she herself had not gone into the library, as that was forbidden, but one of the townsmen had copied it, so I wasn't certain how authentic any of the designs were, whether or not I knew their meanings. Nor it turned out was she.

"I hope the rascal copied this one right," I heard her mumble.

Mostly I enjoyed my task of dyeing the feathers and of studying the splendid designs in those that nature had painted. When I finished that task she gave me a little brush and wanted me to put certain designs onto bark cloth. She said that it was very simple and I'd be able to do it quite easily. I put a painting on them that looked like circles inside circles and other geometric patterns. Only one pattern looked familiar. It resembled my own eyes that Old Xavier had drawn in the sand.

One of the things she made was a sad mask with many-colored feathers sticking out all around it, the eyes oval and slanting down, the mouth slanting down at the corners and huge round balls for ears. Then there was a hat with feathers sticking out around the bottom edges as if there was hair hanging down. There were square patterns in the hat, some painted red, some white, and all made out of straw. She showed me how to weave the pattern into an egg-shaped basket, turned upside down. I was to make many of these hats and attach feathers to them while she made the more difficult mask, with the round ears and cylindrical nose.

On the paper there were animal heads that we'd begin to do tomorrow, she said. My task then would be simply to paint in the little round eyes.

"It's very easy," she said.

I nodded and continued to weave the upside down baskets.

"Will there be any real Indians in the parade?" I asked.

"No, of course not. They're all rascals, didn't I tell you. Just those who claim to have an Indian grandmother or great grandmother here and there. It's not the old days anymore. They all think they've got to celebrate their Indian ancestry instead of condemn it. Even the priest feels it's a good thing."

A picture of Father Tollinare bending to kiss Mexia's hand flashed into my mind, then he turned into the skinny man on the skinny horse and carrying an umbrella.

"Do you have any Indian blood?" I asked, weaving my hat, while watching her attach feathers to one of the bark-cloth masks she'd made.

"No. Haven't I enough defect of blood?"

I looked at her, but she'd spoken casually and automatically, and her face didn't shift from its solemn expression, as she carefully attached feathers, and wiped the moisture from her forehead and around her nose. She didn't even look up at me, or show a familiar smirk to show that we share some feeling. I kept watching her face. Hadn't she called the brancos rascals? Whose defect of blood?

"Look what you're doing."

She pulled the work from my hands. Only a bit of it was twisted in the wrong direction, what I'd done in the past few minutes, because I was very used to watching people while I wove. She took the work apart and then threw it back at me.

"Keep your eyes on what you're doing," she said, a deep frown in her forehead, a line that ran in the middle very deep.

I couldn't read foreheads and tell fortunes in them like my grandmother and Old Vera could, but I felt it had some meaning, and that she must be a woman of some special destiny. The wife of Martim Aprigion had spoken of freedom, but the woman I stared across at was really a free colored woman, and I couldn't help trying to take all of her in, her movements, her turns of phrase.

"Your mother was a slave," I said suddenly, "before he made her a free woman?"

She nodded but did not look up at me.

"Did he marry her to make her free?"

I watched the deep line. Finally, she answered, "No. He declared her a free woman. He declared her and his daughter free. You're a nosey one, eh. He declared us free. I'm his daughter." She looked at me as if to say that if I didn't know that, then I couldn't remember things from one moment to the next.

I was silent, but there were many questions I wanted to ask her about her father and about her mother and about the town that had accepted her as a free woman, colored and all. We worked a whole day before she got up to bring me victuals--a bowl of cabbage and thick and pasty rice with manioc biscuits. Yes, she brought it to me her own self. She didn't say get me this and that. And she herself ate the same, except she didn't give herself manioc biscuits, she ate wheat bread. And I ate in the small room, while she sat in the middle room. She sat facing me, and though I looked into the room at her a great many times, she didn't look at me once.

When we finished eating, I told her how strange it was that she hadn't asked me to prepare the food for herself and me, since it was I who was her servant and she'd rented me.

She said proudly that she'd only gotten me for one task, to help her with the costumes and that she'd continue to do the rest of her work, for she was a woman of honor.

"It's very difficult for a free woman of color in a town such as this one," she said, as she settled down to continue her work.

I started to say that this contradicted what she'd said earlier, but I didn't. I waited for her to continue, but she did not. After some moments I heard a bell ring and she went into the front of the shop. I heard low talking, but couldn't make out any of the words.

When she returned she sat down and said bitterly, "One cannot even dance in the streets with a person of color. My costumes will be in the public procession, but I won't be. Nor did I want to be. I'm mostly a hidden woman, anyway. I'm not a public person. I wouldn't be a public woman, whether I were white or black. A spirit doesn't undergo a change of personality with a change of skin. But to know that I couldn't be even if I chose to. Do you know what I'm saying? There's a free man of color here who's written a play for the public procession. They're making use of his play, but not the man."

She wore an expression that made her look ugly, twisting her mouth almost to the corner of her face. Seeing her like that made me want to turn away, but I continued to watch her. She looked as if she were wearing a mask.

"It's more difficult for him, because his spirit's not so private as my own. Should I wear gloves and one of these sad masks and join the procession anyway, Almedya?"

I didn't know she knew my name. She said it wrong, but I didn't correct her.

"Should I make a mask for him, and we both go that way?"

She waited as if I'd had an answer, but what could I say?

"Even the tooth puller's daughter will dance in the streets next week." She bowed her head and examined one of the masks. She still wore her own mask. "But I'm not a dancing woman, nor a public one, and I'd be a hidden woman whether white or black."

Her expression grew easier, and she took up more bark cloth, and began to create another mask for the people who'd take part in the procession, and who'd changed their names to Indian names for trees and rivers.

I wondered about the man she'd mentioned and what their relationship was, and if they loved each other. When she'd mentioned what they'd do, I saw a masked man and woman dancing along the streets.

We worked for several more hours in silence, then she leaned back in her chair and breathed heavily. She lined up several of the sad-faced masks in front of her on the table, then pushing them away, she put her forehead down on the table.

"Are you married?" I asked.

She raised her head and straightened her shoulders.

"No," she replied, but the tone of her voice sounded proud, even of that. Then she rose slowly and reaching into a corner, she got a folded hammock. "Here, hold this end."

I got up and held it. She tied one end to a hooked post sticking out of the wall, then she took the end I was holding and tied it to the hook sticking from the other wall. Coming back around the table, she almost stumbled, but reaching out, caught the table. I rushed to catch her, but she'd already braced herself against the table. I stood awkwardly, watching her.

"You sleep in here," she said, coming around me and standing in the arched doorway between the two rooms.

She seemed suddenly very nervous and almost afraid of me.

"You've done very good work," she said. "I probably won't need you for more than a couple of more days."

"Are they paying you for your work?" I asked, not knowing why I asked it.

She frowned. "No, everyone's contributing. Everyone who has a business is contributing something."

"How much did I cost?"

"What?"

"To rent me. How much was I?"

"That's none of your concern."

I pushed myself up into the hammock, still staring at her.

"Don't look at me with such eyes," she said.

I looked away from her. When I looked again the doorway was empty. I heard her climb into her own hammock.

I stayed with her for several more days, attaching feathers to the masks she made and painting eyes on animal heads.

"What was he like?" I asked her once.

"Which he?"

"Your father. The carpenter. And your mother too. What kind of woman?" I finally got my questions out.

"And am I to tell you? Am I to tell you that?" She looked at me with narrowed eyes. "You're such a talkative creature, and nosey too. I don't like talkative creatures with their noses everywhere. If you want to grow to be a good woman, learn to be silent and mind your own business."

"I usually don't talk very much, but I'm always curious."

She smiled at me, then she straightened her shoulders. "But with me, eh? You think because you're looking at your same color, there's no distance between us, and that I'm the same as you, and have no right to demand your respectful silence."

She tied the string of her trousers, then she tied her breasts very tightly, and put on a loose white shirt. She put a cream on her lips that took a slightly berry-color away from them, then she pushed her hair up and put the large white hat on, down across her forehead.

"How do I look?"

"Like a man," I said glumly.

"But I can't change my voice, there's nothing I can do to change my voice. So I pretend he's mute."

"Oh."

"Don't be angry with me. I accept my station the same as I accept my defect of blood."

I said nothing. But again she'd spoken without changing her expression or looking at me as if we shared some special knowledge.

"I'm no tooth puller's daughter," she said, looking perfectly like a man, with the hat making a long shadow on her face. "No, and my father was more than a carpenter. The sculptured figures for the church he made, and many churches in the territory. If he'd stayed in the Old World and hadn't come to the New, he'd have sculptured different art. You'd have seen his work in galleries. I'm no teeth puller's daughter. Don't look at me like that....You think because we share the same blood...." She looked at me haughtily from under her straw hat. "No, don't assume that, and even if I were a white woman I'd be the same one you see here, hidden in these rooms. I'd be the same woman you see standing here now. Don't think we share anything of the spirit because we share the same blood. And don't ask me again of that man and woman either. Don't ask me anything about them, because it's not your place to."

I followed her outside and climbed into the back of the wagon. When we returned to Azevedo's plantation, Old Xavier was sitting on the ground outside his hut with his bottles arranged in front of him. The woman drove the wagon right up to him.

"Tell Mascarenhas I returned her," she said in her own woman's voice.

Xavier nodded but said nothing. I climbed out of the wagon, but still stood near them.

"Climb down, Maria," he said, as if she were someone he'd known a very long time.

She did as she was told and sat on the ground near him.

"Nyanga," he called her.

He ran his hand along her forehead and the side of her neck and pushed his hand in the air as if he were shaking something away from her. Then he lifted one of the bottles that lay beside him and handed it to her.

"That will relieve the ailment," he said.

She thanked him and stood up. She looked at me with what seemed to be embarrassment, then she climbed onto the driver's seat and drove away.

I kept staring down at Old Xavier, wondering what it was he'd given her.

"Do you believe it is only bodily ailments that Old Xavier treats?" he inquired. "Don't you think his territory is also the spirit? Don't you think he treats ailments of the soul?"

I said nothing, because that was the answer I'd given myself, that this time he'd given a remedy for the soul.

Suddenly my legs began to tremble and I fell to the ground in front of him. I felt as though I couldn't move, felt as if I'd been drugged. I saw him placing flowers and beads on the ground in front of me.

"Accept these offerings and take them to your jeweled home in the sea."

He kept watching me, although I couldn't straighten or stand. I stared into his copper brown eyes. The sky behind him looked as if it were lit by candles. Then he held large banana leaves and began to rub them all over my face and body.

"Are you an African woman?" he asked.

"I am the granddaughter of an African," I replied.

"You are the same as any woman except when the spirit of one of the gods enters. But tell me, are you an informer? Are you a spy who has been sent here to ferret out the hiding place of these renegades?"

I answered him as if I knew exactly what he was saying and why and said, "No."

"You are not?"

"No."

"Well, they hanged him and put his head on a pole as a warning to the other rebels. That he is no immortal man."

"Oh, yes, he is immortal, as his soul has come into all of us."

"Are you a woman alone?"

"Yes, in the beginning. They attacked a small town and then the plantation and declared us free."

"Were you afraid?"

"Yes, but I trust fear. No one has the right to determine the liberty of others. To make them free or to keep them from freedom."

"Are you any other woman?"

"I'm Almedya." I said my name wrong, then I corrected it. "Almeyda."

Then the Indian woman was standing there, rising above me, candles in the sky behind her.

"The whole right side of her face looks swollen. May I lift her up?"

"No."

"Do you think it's erysipelas?"

"No."

"May I lift her up?"

"Where?"

"Into my bosom. She sought protection in an Indian village, but the Indians themselves captured her."

"Was it this one?"

"Perhaps this one."

"No, they were protecting us," I said. "I was riding on his shoulders. His helmet was made of anteater's skin."

Xavier kept rubbing the banana leaves all over my face and body, and then he lifted cassava branches, scraping them all over me.

"Is it an ailment of the spirit or of the soul?" asked the Indian woman.

"He gave her biscuits and a pair of shoes and so she informed on the hiding place of the rebels."

"No!" I shouted. "No!"

Xavier kept scraping the cassava branches up and down my back and thighs, my whole body twisted, my face turned up to him.

"Did you see her in the Holy Week procession?"

"Yes, and they don't allow colored women."

"It's difficult for a colored woman to live in such a town," I said.

"Do you trust fear?"

"Yes."

"Did you make a mask?"

"I put feathers along the edges of them."

"Did you see the man who came to visit me? He's the godfather of my child."

"Father?"

"Godfather."

"Barbacoeba's his name. He came first and stayed with the wife of Martim Aprigio and then he saw me and knelt down and said he'd never seen such a beautiful woman. He didn't know where such beautiful women came from in such a country. Aren't you the enchanted Mooress, your lips tinted with berries, the blue of the sky on your eyelids?"

I couldn't tell if I was the one speaking or the Indian woman.

"Lips tinted with blood?" asked Xavier.

"It's not only my people who've made such sacrifices or have come into strange lands to live off the flesh and blood of others. Oh, it's the gods who rest on the old stones and know everything. I'm a silent woman in the worst country. Why does she look at me with such eyes?"

"Why does she look at us with such eyes?" Xavier repeated.

"Has she come to solve the mystery of this place?"

"Only the gods rest on the stones and know everything. You have said it."

"Look how her shoes are wide open."

"I'm not wearing any."

"Why does she look at us so?"

"Yemanja? Is this the goddess Yemanja?"

"I'm Almeyda. Didn't I say so?"

"Have you shown her how to rise up out of her body? Have you presented her with a supernatural gift?"

"It's only the gods who sit on the stones and know everything."

He kept rubbing cassava branches on me, till the leaves had broken off, then he lay the naked branches on the ground beside me. My body sore, and blood raised in places.

"Any man can raise blood," said the Indian woman. "But have you shown her the other?"

Xavier placed an amulet around my neck, an amulet made of seeds and trumpet shells. He rubbed an oil over my arms and thighs and the wounds healed. What was left, he lifted my head and made me drink. I rose into the sky, floating above the candles. Then when I was back beside them lying on the banana and cassava leaves, they lifted me and carried me into the long hut where the women were and lay me on my hammock. They carried me easily, for I was very light.

"The next time I come I'll come in a form that will please you," he said, and he bent and kissed my mouth.

Xavier and the Indian woman walked away. I lay there. Then the old woman Vera was standing silent above me. I tried to raise up, but couldn't. Though the scratches on my body were healed, I could still feel the sting of them.

"They say that we're rivals but we're not," she confided. "We work together."

I said nothing.

"He won't keep you very long now," she said.

"Who?"

She laughed hard.

"Azevedo," she said. "Does anyone else make such a decision here?"

I still couldn't move and stared up at her. Then I asked, "Why won't he keep me?"

"Because he's afraid of what you know, afraid of what you saw, afraid you'll tell me. He's afraid of me knowing it. It's less you than me he fears."

Her eyes got larger, rounder. She had a habit of widening her eyes at certain times when she spoke to someone. And when she did it it was like a light, a spark or a spirit jumped out from them. Now the light jumped out. I shut my eyes, to avoid her penetrating stare.

"But didn't you already see?" I asked.

"Yes, I *see*." I could still feel her above me. "He thinks I don't see what he's come to, that I don't know. He thinks only he sees this old woman, peeking out of his slit. He thinks I can't see the man that's in that covered hammock. Every way he hides himself from me, but do you think I can't see?"

I wanted to see the eyes of the woman now, but dared not open my eyes to look at her. She began to laugh again, but then grew very silent.

"He thinks you'll repeat what he said of me. Does he fear that? As if I couldn't repeat him word for word and sentence by sentence, nor tell you every rise and fall of his voice. Every rise and fall of his voice. He thinks I didn't see that? He thinks I can't see him now, eh? He's never hidden from this woman. No. I see what you saw with your own eyes that day, and more than you saw. Do you hear me? I see what you saw with your own eyes and more. Strange symbols he'd put on paper and say that was his science. Strange symbols I'd write on the ground, and say that was mine. Should I tell you my story? Should I make my case?"

I opened my eyes and looked at her.

"He says I'm one of the witches they brought from Africa, but I won't claim anything. Should I say I wasn't even there when the fire started? Well, I was healing someone, burning coca leaves to rid a young girl of demons, rubbing ash on her eyelids. He claimed he saw me running away from the house. Others claimed they saw me too. But wasn't I there, forcing the young girl to stare into the fire?"

I nodded.

"Telling her she was a new woman, telling her over and over again she was not the same, burning coca leaves, forcing the girl to be a new woman. Wasn't I curing someone?"

I nodded again.

"But he says he saw me and that I leaped into the air and ran as fast as a serpent. And how could I be two places at one time? How could I be curing that girl and destroying him in his house at the same time? Didn't the girl see me? Didn't I force the smoke into her nostrils and paint her eyelids? So I'm one of the witches that came from Africa, eh, but didn't I cure that girl?"

I nodded yet again.

"Didn't I share some of the knowledge of the heavens with her? How, then, can I be in two places at one time?"

Did I sleep? I opened my eyes and she was not there but there was the smell of burning coca leaves.

The Shoemaker and the Sadism of the Senhora

"Did you rent me or buy me?" I dared to ask the silent Sobrieski.

He said nothing as we walked across a banana grove toward a long squat building. Near it under palm trees were three slave huts, smaller and not as well constructed as the ones on Azevedo's plantation--though this could not rightly be called a plantation.

"I have only two other slaves," he said, though it did not seem as if he were speaking to me, but I walked slightly behind him and so could not see his eyes.

"I work hard like a slave myself," he said.

He certainly dressed like one, I was thinking. I waited for him to go on talking but he said nothing.

As we drew near the buildings, I thought he would point to one of the huts for me to enter, but instead he kept walking and I followed him into the back doorway of the long squat building--that I later learned was both his house and workshop. As soon as we got inside I saw two slaves sitting at a long wooden table covered with straps of leather. Lined along the walls were sandals and high top European shoes. One of the men, who was sewing leather into a cylindrical shape looked up at me. The other, who was pounding leather and had sandals piled up to the side of him, did not. In one corner were piled saddle bags, but I saw only one saddle, a very expensive-looking one among the rows of shoes.

Sobrieski went inside, but I stayed in the doorway.

"Sit down," he said.

"Capao, show her how to string the sandals," he said to the man who was pounding leather.

Capao looked at me grimly and stopped what he was doing.

I sat down in one of the chairs near him, but not very close.

"Sit here," Capao said.

I sat closer. Sobrieski left the workshop and disappeared in the next room.

Capao took a flat piece of leather and a long strap. Holes were already in the leather, so I did not have to worry about that.

"Here and here and here," he said simply, showing me what to do, then tying the end of the strap, and pulling it tightly in his teeth.

"Do you see how to do it?" he asked.

I nodded. He handed the other one to me, then watched as I made his movements, though not so quickly as he did, and finished by pulling the string between my teeth, except that it felt that my teeth also were being pulled, as I was not used to using them in labors.

He laughed.

"What?" I asked.

"You squinch up your face so. You put all your face into it."

"There," I said, putting it down.

"Good," he said, pushing a pile of flat bottoms of different shapes and sizes over to me, and a bundle of straps. "That is your job now."

He went back to his pounding and stretching leather.

I did another one. At the end of several, my teeth felt as if they were out of my mouth. I told him so.

He handed me a metal clamp. "Here, put it in here." Then he pulled on it.

"Better?" he asked.

I nodded.

He went back to his work.

"Am I being rented or did he buy me?" I asked Capao.

"How should I know? I am a slave the same as you. Do you think the master shares his business transactions with me?"

"Well, do you know how long I will be here?"

"Forever? And what business would it be of yours or mine?"

I started to say something, but he rapped the table in front of me.

"He likes silence from his workers. Do you want to get in trouble on your first day?"

I said nothing. I pulled one of the flat soles toward me and strung it.

After I had completed those, he tossed them into a corner, and showed me the proper stitching for more intricate looking shoes.

"You learn very quickly," he said.

I pricked my finger and there was a bloodstain on the leather. I wiped it away on the back of my hand. There were footsteps and then silence.

Sobrieski looked over my shoulder.

"Not so far apart," he said. He grabbed what I was doing, stitched and returned it.

I stitched again. He said nothing, watched me a while longer, then went into a corner of the workshop, sat at a desk, on which were saddle bags. He dipped into a bowl and began to rub some kind of oil on them. Every now and then he would get up and stare over my shoulder, but would say nothing. In his corner, he began to cut shapes into huge pieces of leather. The man sitting next to Capao, and who had said nothing the whole time I was there, began to sew buttons into the thick leather.

I felt her before I saw her--a woman holding a baby and standing in the door. I looked back at her and I was the one she was looking at hard. I looked back at the work I was doing, but I still felt her eyes on my back. I pricked my finger again, staining the leather. Capao glanced over at me, but said nothing. He had begun his stitching now, more complicated and intricate than my own. He slid a very black cloth over to me, for me to wipe the leather. The woman still stood in the doorway and then I heard a strange sound. I glanced back and saw that she had undone her blouse and taken one of her breasts out and the baby was sucking on it. She had a strange look on her face as she watched me--for it was me she continued to watch and no one else, as if I were the only one in the room and even her husband was not there. Her hair was a very pale and flimsy brown and I could not tell what her strange expression must mean. None of the men turned to look at her, not even her husband, who continued to cut pieces of leather. After some moments, though probably fewer than it seemed, I turned back to what I was doing. She was very much younger than Sobrieski. She seemed to be in her mid twenties while he appeared to be in his early forties. I do not know the meaning of the woman's look or the very slight smile that was on her lips--but it was not the kind of smile one takes for kindness or interest, but a very slight though self-conscious smile that made me afraid of her.

Then my fingers were slapped and Sobrieski grabbed the leather from me. He took a pen knife from his pocket and slit the stitches I had made, made several stitches, then tossed the leather sandal back on the table.

I turned and saw the woman, still eyeing me--a deeper smirk.

"Agostinha," Sobrieski said.

She disappeared from the doorway. We worked again in silence until the woman placed bowls of rice and cassava in front of us and banana leaves to roll the mixture in. Then we stopped and Sobrieski disappeared into the exterior of the house.

"She fears you," Capao said.

"What?"

"Don't you see the woman is afraid of you," he said. "She wonders what her husband might come to see in you, and so she is afraid."

I said nothing. Then I said, "I am afraid of her."

"For what reason?" he asked.

"The way she was looking at me. I was afraid of her."

"Then we have two women who are afraid of each other," Capao said as if he were making a joke.

I stared down into my bowl of rice and cassava.

"I am afraid of that woman," I said.

Capao sat stroking his forehead and saying nothing. He touched my shoulder. I pulled away from him.

"Aren't you more afraid of the man than you are of the woman?" he asked.

I said nothing, then I said I was not afraid of any man, and he began to laugh.

"How are you doing, Pedro the Third?" he asked the man next to him.

Pedro nodded, but said nothing.

"Pedro the Third won't speak to anyone. He stays silent. He thinks that silence will free him." Capao chuckled.

Pedro the Third took a handful of rice and ate it in glum silence.

"Who knows why he is called Pedro the Third?" Capao said. "Neither his father nor his father before him has had such a name. Why is he not Pedro the First?"

I looked at Pedro the Third who scraped his fingers with his teeth.

"Do you know why he is in such a state?" Capao asked.

I shook my head no.

"Because he fought against his own kind, that's why. He was in the military, in another territory, and they sent him on expeditions against escaped Negroes. And he captured many, many, and informed on many."

He waited for me to speak, but I was silent.

"They decorated him for all the niggers he has captured. Ha. Ha, but now he is a slave himself. The niggers captured him and cut out his tongue and put an 'f' on his forehead, for fugitive. And that is why you see him in the condition that he's in today."

Pedro the Third did not look at either one of us. And there was silence for a very long time. I thought of the evil that the man had done and the evil that had been done to him.

"How do you know all this if he has not spoken?" I asked.

"It was I who put the 'f' on my own forehead," Pedro the Third said. "I painted 'f' on my own forehead."

Capao began to laugh. I did not like the joke that had been played.

"Are you still afraid of the woman?" Capao said.

"I am afraid of no one," I said glumly.

When Sobrieski returned I sewed in glum silence. When it was time to go outside I followed Capao and Pedro the Third. Sobrieski did not go with us. I had expected that all three of us would have a hut, but Capao and Pedro the Third walked into the same one. I stayed standing outside. When I did not follow them in, Capao came outside.

"What are you doing?"

"Waiting to be told where I'm to sleep."

"There are three hammocks hanging in this one," he said, pointing to the one he had just entered. "There is red meat hanging in that one, and in the other tanned hide. What will it be? Choose as you wish."

He went back inside. Silently I followed him.

After I had been there a week, the wife of Sobrieski asked her husband why couldn't I do chores for her while the men did chores for him. She could not understand why he had me in there with the men and I was never getting any stitches right; she said why couldn't I help her, with the laundry and the housework and other things that were women's work.

I did not hear her say these things of course but soon it was that in the mornings I would do the things she wanted done, taking the laundry down to the stream, baking cassava bread, polishing the rosewood furniture with coconut oil. She would only speak to me to tell me what thing it was she wanted me to do, and she would always find a great many things, and sometimes I felt that she was putting clean clothes in with the dirty ones. In the afternoon my hands would be shaking from the work she had demanded. Then there were more occasions where Sobrieski would slap my fingers, and she would stand in the doorway smirking with the baby sucking at her breast. But again in the day, I would say nothing to her and she would say nothing to me except to make her orders of my chores for the morning.

Once when I was down at the stream washing clothes I heard footsteps and there she was, coming toward me and carrying a basket. I thought she was bringing more work but she set the basket down away from me, upstream, but I could see the top of the baby's head and hear his sleeping noises. She stood there beside the baby, away from me, and not saying anything, looking out into the clear water as if she were contemplating something.

Then she began slowly to undress, first taking off her top garments, so that her large breasts dropped out, then she took off the rest of her clothes. She swam, she played, she bathed. I continued to wash the clothes, the dirty ones and what looked like clean garments. Then she was suddenly up there beside me, her light hair out about her shoulders, her white shoulders and breasts out of the water.

"Almeyda, it's nice in here," she said. "Why don't you take your clothes off and join me. There's room enough for two women."

I did not know why she said the last thing she did the way she said it.

"This is how I used to see the Indian women bathing," she said, "looking like enchanted Moors."

"Come and get in," she said, looking at me now with hard eyes. "It's so comfortable. One feels as if one's whole spirit is being healed."

She stayed in front of me, till I could no longer scrub clothes.

"I'll bet you'd look just like them, just like an enchanted Moorish woman," she said. "I bet you'd look just like them. Come and get in the water. Do you want me to pull you in? Do you want me to tell my husband that you won't behave? Do you want him to beat you?"

Slowly I began to take my clothes off as she watched me.

"You look just like them," she said, as I stepped into the water. She kept her eyes on me. "You look like an enchanted Moorish woman like in the storybook. Except your hair's not long, except your hair's so awfully short."

Her own hair was floating on the water now.

"I always wanted black hair," she said. "Like the woman in the storybook. But my husband likes my hair, he does. I'm not a Polish woman. I'm a full-blooded Portuguese woman," she said proudly.

I said nothing. I had not gone far into the water, but stayed with my back against the bank.

"Doesn't it feel as if your spirit is being healed?" she asked.

I did not answer. Again she played, and swam, and sprinkled water on her breasts and arms. Then she was in front of me again and turned her back to me and sat in the water.

"I've got lice in my hair. I think there's lice in my hair," she said.

I put my fingers to her loose hair and searched for lice.

Then I felt a sharp stone glaze my thigh. I reached down and grabbed my thigh as she sprang from the water and the water reddened. I turned to see her tossing her clothes into the basket with the baby and running into the forest, disappearing. Still holding my thigh I climbed into the water, and sat against the bank. I washed the leg. It was a long but not a very deep cut. I tore some of the linen and wrapped it. I put on my clothes and rinsed the few pieces that were left. I started to throw the torn undergarment into the stream, but instead put it back in the basket. Near the house, I flung everything onto low branches to dry in the sun and wind.

When I finished I walked into the hut but not knowing there was blood on my dress.

"Is it your time?" Capao asked, when Sobrieski was not present.

"What?"

"There's blood stains on your dress. What goes?"

I was silent.

"What goes, woman?"

"I cut myself on a stone," I said. "When I was down at the stream. I fell against a stone."

"Where?" he asked, frowning.

"Just my thigh. It's not very bad. It doesn't hurt."

He said nothing.

"Did she send you to wash the laundry and her hair?"

"What?"

"I saw the woman coming back with wet hair."

I said nothing. He looked at me. I looked away.

"I'll make a salve for you to put on it," he said, and went back to his work. "Cuts can be dangerous."

I said nothing, and stitched the leather with shaking fingers.

This time I did not think she would appear but she did, holding the baby against her breasts and watching my back. Had she tried to raise the stone higher? I wondered. Did she know it was only a scratch on my thigh or had she done me some greater harm?

She left the doorway and came back without the baby. Her hair, still damp, was down about her shoulders. She started to brush it.

Her husband did not look back at her. I continued sewing the thick leather.

The next time I was alone with her she held a piece of broken glass. I was in the kitchen, wringing the moisture out of cassava paste, getting ready to bake it. I felt her and turned and she was holding a piece of broken glass.

"This is a devil of a thing," she said. "My husband ordered me a pretty glass vase from Lisbon, and it arrived broken. I thought I'd gotten all of it up. But this is really a devil of a thing. I'm glad the baby didn't crawl onto it. In my own country, glass seems so pretty, but here it just seems a devil of a thing."

She went to dispose of it, but each day I waited to feel the cut across my face, or the slash in some more secret place, but nothing happened, nor did she come down to the stream again. But each afternoon she would stand in the doorway while her baby sucked at her breast, and after she put him down, she would begin the new thing--brushing her long hair. Had it been her threat to show what she would do to me if given any reason? Yet if she did fear that her husband would take notice of me, it was needless, for he went about his shop as if I were not there, the same way he went about it in her presence, yet she would continue to watch me as if I were the only one in the room, and as if her husband were in some danger of my charms.

Once a day Sobrieski would stand and watch our hands as we worked. If something was done wrong, he would slap the fingers that did it or rap the table. Always, I was the only one who would sometimes put a stitch wrong. And as Capao had said he expected us to observe silence as he himself did when he worked. For Pedro the Third it was no burden, as he neither talked when Sobrieski was there or away. And at night when we lay in our hammocks, he spoke not a word.

But there was one time when Capao drove into the city with Sobrieski to take a wagonload of shoes to be sold in a shop there, and as we continued to work in silence, Pedro the Third said, "Do you wonder why this man stopped talking?"

"You have told me," I said. "That you informed on your own people and captured them."

"And performed all horrible cruelties against them without once seeing my own face. I was in Portuguese service. They were not my own people. I did not see my own face anywhere among them."

"Did the white men turn on you and make you a slave after you had served them?"

"No. I made myself a slave."

"You made yourself?"

"I did not go into the military thinking that it would be fugitive slaves I would be sent after. No. First we were promised our freedom if we would enlist, and what did I think? I imagined exploring all parts of the world unknown, and what if there was danger? It was the places unknown. But what places unknown!" He thumped his head and then his heart. "Here and here."

Then again he was silent and continued to go his days without saying one word to me or to anyone in my hearing.

Mr. Iaiyesimi

A black man stood in the doorway, and a woman stood shy behind him. They were both dressed in expensive European clothes. The man was very large with broad shoulders and very dark smooth skin, and the woman's skin was dark and soft and was very delicate looking, but she wouldn't come from behind the man.

Sobrieski did not see them as he sat in the corner, but then he saw them and got up hurriedly.

"Are you…" he began.

"I am Mr. Iaiyesimi."

He stood stiffly and spoke with dignity. I'd never seen such a man and I thought of the one the wife of Martim Aprigio had spoken of and imagined this was him. It was only years later that I discovered that this was indeed him and that they were not what they seemed, but spies for the rebels. Then, however, I simply stared at them like they were curiosities.

Although Mr. Iaiyesimi spoke to Sobrieski, he didn't look at him, but over his shoulder at me.

"Yes, yes," said Sobrieski. I had never seen him behave so excitedly. He began to make exaggerated motions with his hand.

"Mr. Sobrieski?"

"Yes, yes." He ushered them inside. The woman still lingered behind.

"Come in Zaria."

Sobrieski took them over to his desk. Mr. Iaiyesimi was carrying a box that he set down on the desk.

"This is not your concern," Sobrieski said, and we went back to work.

"There are the bark cloth shoes that my company makes. And this is vegetable fibre."

"You say it holds even in a rainy climate?"

"Yes. These I'll leave with you. We've purchased a shop in Porto Calvo, and have taken a house there."

I felt as if he were looking at me and when I turned he was, as was also the woman, who stood shyly near her husband. I looked down at the work I was doing--embroidery work on a pair of special sandals for a rich woman in Porto Calvo.

"What house have you rented?" asked Sobrieski.

"The house and shop both from a Dutchman named Lantz."

"Oh, yes. What do you think of our town of Porto Calvo?" Sobrieski spoke to him as if he were a white man.

Mr. Iaiyesimi was silent.

"My wife and I, they laughed at us until they found out we were of royal blood in another country and that I'm the owner of much land and many factories and many slaves. Now we're treated with respect suitable to our position. By those who know. Mainly the town's businessmen, of course."

"Yes, yes," said Sobrfieski.

"But it's of little consequence. I don't think my wife and I will spend very long in this place, to suffer the insults of strangers. But eventually we'll get a white man to manage it, although sometimes it's taken me moments of ponder to decide who is who in this land."

He looked at me then, although I was certain that I couldn't be mistaken for anything else. Besides him and his wife, though, my skin seemed to take on a lighter shade, but beside Sobrieski's it seemed as dark as anyone's.

"This country is not unlike my own, Sir, as far as the climate goes, and what I hope to do is to introduce certain building materials as well as my shoe manufacturing. Because these Dutch houses are nonsense. But I don't feel it will be accepted. 'It's not Africa, Sir,' said one of the fellows. 'But neither is it Portugal or Holland,' I told him. Or better, it's France or England they want to see here. My wife and I come into the city and it's not Mr. Iaiyesimi and his wife they see, but buffoons and clowns. And they're surprised at how tender and shy my wife Zaria is."

"Who is this woman?" he asked, pointing at me.

Sobrieski looked uncomfortable, then he explained that I was one of his servants, one of his slaves.

"In my country, she would be a woman of quality," said Mr. Iaiyesimi.

He continued to look at me, and so did his wife, while Sobrieski stood by with a look of much discomfort.

"So, they see my black face, they think it is the same one they see here," said Mr. Iaiyesimi, still looking at me as if the two men Capao and Pedro the Third were not there. Pedro continued his work in silence. Capao continued his with a frown.

"Well, she looks fierce and intelligent enough," said Mr. Iaiyesimi, with a deep sigh. Then he turned to his own woman and clasped her shoulder. She still looked at me, but with shy curiosity and not like most women whose husband had spoken of another woman in such a way. "Well, Zaria, if my plans were not unsettled I would purchase her for you. What would you say to that?"

Zaria nodded. I did not know the meaning of it all then, as Mr. Iaiyesimi turned to Sobrieski. "Mr. Sobrieski, it's been a pleasure," he said, with a slight bow. "Please let me know your decision about the matter."

Sobrieski shook his hand and nodded, but now he was looking at them with curiosity and confusion. Mr. Iaiyesimi left without explaining anything.

"Get back to work, you," said Sobrieski.

Men From the Quilombo

As I sat cutting and sewing leather, I thought I heard the scream of a woman. I don't know why, but I pictured the Indian woman with her back on the ground, then I pictured Mr. Iaiyesimi's shy and tender wife, Zaria. Then I saw the man again at the cassava barn shielding his eyes from the fire as he opened the small door to put more wood into the furnace. I saw the tall woman holding cassava bread over the furnace. All the women's arms were white with cassava flour, the white rising past their elbows, their hands sticky and white. I saw Azevedo with his machete. Then everyone looked to the door.

Four black men stood in the doorway, two holding knives, one a sword, one a musket. I was the first to see them. The man holding the musket steadied it at me. I was silent. Then Capao and Pedro saw. Sobrieski saw and remained at his table, although he looked quickly at the direction his wife might be, but she was not standing here. I wondered how the scene might have been if she'd been standing there with the baby at her breast.

"Who else is here?" demanded the man holding the musket.

"There is a white woman and a baby," I said.

"Araujo, go see."

Araujo went into the next room and came back, the woman walking in front of him and holding the baby. She looked frightened, and for the first time did not look at me.

"Do you wish to come freely with us and be free men and a free woman?" the man with the musket asked. "For if you do not come freely, you'll be slaves wherever you go."

No one said anything.

"It is to Palmares," Pedro said knowingly.

The man with the musket said nothing, then he came and took my arm.

"Do you go with me of your own will?" he asked.

"Yes," I answered.

He told the men to follow if it was their will. Capao stood but Pedro the Third remained sitting.

"Araujo," said the man, still holding my arm tightly.

Araujo put the sword under Pedro's chin.

"Come. And it is not to your freedom that you go."

The two men had tied Sobrieski and the woman with leather straps and lay the baby on the table on a pile of soles.

We followed them, walking in a column. Two of the Palmares men were in the lead, two others behind us. Araujo held the sword to Pedro's back. As we walked through the dense forest over tangled vines and palm leaves, I kept waiting for signs of blood, but saw none. We marched through the heavy forest, everyone as silent as Pedro.

When we arrived at the place called Palmares, I saw the old woman Vera, and two of the younger women from Azevedo's plantation, one being the wife of Martim Aprigio. It was the old woman Vera who winked at me. When I got close to the old woman, I asked her what happened and why hadn't more come to be free here. She said that Mascarenhas had been killed, and the men who'd not wanted to come they had murdered. After that, I wondered why they hadn't murdered Pedro. She said that Pita had come and the Fazendo had stayed.

"Did they kill Fazendo?" I asked.

"No."

"You us said they…."

"Fazendo said that he wanted to stay with his woman."

"His woman? What woman?"

"The Indian woman."

My eyes widened.

"And Azevedo. Is he dead?"

She laughed, then she said, "I wasn't there, but I'm told that they went through his mansion taking everything they wanted, gold, silver, provisions, arms, and ammunition. All he did was sit in his hammock and watch them. He said nothing, but I'm told that he asked them to finish him and perhaps that's why they didn't, because he asked them to, because it was his will. And when they refused, he asked them to send him lararaca, send him the mystical serpent, send him that one to stare on him and finish him."

Her eyes widened, and the light jumped out. The man, Pedro, who'd refused to come was marched off before the rest of us.

"He wasn't killed," I said to Vera. "He refused to come and they didn't kill him."

"Didn't they kill him?" she asked.

We still stood at the entrance where the caltrops and spiked pieces of wood rose up from the ground. They hadn't yet taken us into the village surrounded by palm forests, but we could see the many large and small huts and many comfortable and fine-looking houses, and a large palace where we were told the King Zumbi lived. And there were gardens and fields. We stood there for what seemed like hours, the man with the musket standing near us, and another standing on a high rock looking down on us. At the edge of the village was a very high cliff that dropped down. When we entered, they didn't take us very far when we were told to sit down in a circle and we made sort of a camp at the entrance to the village. I tried to breathe in being a free woman, as I was told would happen here, but instead I felt uncertainty and danger, although in the distance I saw only black men and women and a few Indians walking about. I stare at the banana groves.

Food was brought to us by a very tall broad-shouldered woman. She was silent as she walked among us, and she looked at no one as she bent from the shoulder to hand us the dishes of onions, baked fish, rice, cassava bread, fried bananas, coconut and fresh cow's milk, which I do not remember ever having, and did not like its taste, but drank it as I was very thirsty. I kept staring at the woman who served us with lowered eyes. She was dressed not unlike us, but in the distance there were some men and women dressed in Portuguese and Dutch clothes, some which I later learned were spoils from their raids, while others were from an ordinary and quite regular trade they carried on with certain Pernambucans. This, of course, was not official and was in defiance of the laws and of the government which had resolved to destroy Palmares. Many Pernambucans, I learned, sent their slaves as agents to trade with us or they themselves met with the Palmares agents. These Pernambucans were in that way also protected from our raids.

But I did not know all that then, and it was too early for me to speak of "us" and "ours." I spit out the cow's milk, and grabbed a coconut.

The man with the musket was soon relieved by a man with a bow and arrow. However, he was dressed in a Portuguese military uniform, which made me want to smile, though I kept my face without any expression.

Then I lifted up the coconut and drank.

"Palmares."

. . . .

I thought of Father Tollenare's question years ago about what my true place was in the world.

"Do you think you'll find your spiritual place in this world?"

"Palmares!" I shouted. Then I whispered to the woman beside me, "Who is that pacha?"

"Pacha? Why that's King Zumbi. That's Zumbi himself. That's Zumbi himself. That's the king of Palmares himself."

"Don't talk to me of kings," said another of the women. "It's freedom I want to hear."

"Then you've come to the right place," I said. "For Palmares and freedom are the same."

"Come? Come? Come? Did you say?" asked another. "Why, they dragged me here. Is that what freedom is?"

I lifted up the coconut and drank.